Songbird

By Angeleen Fraser

Songbird

Copyright © 2014
Angeleen Fraser
LC Stassen

Cover: Domhnulla D, www.raksincendia.com

Cover photo: Shutterstock

Other Books by Angeleen Fraser

-Kye & Daphne: Part One

Dedication

To A.D.O. for the jumpstart of inspiration and that terrible song with my name in it.

Kat, my best friend, soul sister, and dance partner. I love you to the moon and back.

Ellen (Georgiana), my sister witch, anam cara, and fellow writer. Your insights, guidance, and filthy conversations were invaluable to me during this process.

Stacy, thank you for being my cheerleader. Your unending enthusiasm every time I had new pages for you to read gave me the motivation I needed to keep going! Love you!

Christine, thank you for volunteering to proofread for me. Your expertise, honesty, and pervy remarks were just what I needed! Mu-wah!

Mr. D, my partner in life. I love you, my winemaking rock star. Thank you for accepting my habit of admiring shirtless men on television...and then writing about them. Ahem.

Prologue

Tulsa, Oklahoma – 7 years ago

"I don't understand, Aydo." I was sitting sideways on the bench seat of his beat up old Bronco with my back resting against the door.

He wouldn't look at me. His knuckles were white as he gripped the steering wheel.

"I don't know what there is to understand, Luce. I want to break up, there's nothing more to say."

My face and ears were hot, my palms sweating as the ball of dread and misery unfurled in my gut. *No,* I thought. *We're so happy...how can this be?*

"You're lying to me, Adrien. I don't know what's going on with you or why you're doing this, but I know there's more to it than what you're saying." I had a dismal internal celebration that I hadn't yet shed a tear.

He eyes remained focused on my garage door as he stared out the windshield, "Goodbye, Luce."

I could have sworn I heard tears in *his* voice, but I didn't really care as I burned with a searing anger and had to get out of his truck. Back stiff, I walked to my front door and leaned my forehead against the cool metal trying to compose myself before I had to face my dad.

I nearly leaped out of my skin when Aydo's hands closed around my upper arms.

He's taking it back! I thought happily until I turned around and looked up into his face. His eyes were shiny and looked wet, but his countenance remained hard and blank.

Without a word, he pressed a lingering kiss against my forehead, then jumped into his Bronco and sped off.

That's the moment I crumbled.

1

Tulsa, Oklahoma – Present day

Once upon a time, I found myself back in Tulsa.

Fuck, it was hot. I missed my cool, comfortable house in Oregon.

My belly dance sister, Nova, and I were on a tour with a few other groups of musicians, dance soloists and troupes for the summer. By some cosmic fuckery, we ended up in Tulsa. Okla-fucking-homa. It reaches over 100 degrees there in the summer...I should know, I lived there for four long years of high school.

And here I was standing outside Cain's Ballroom, burning alive. Any moment now, I would burst into flames...was that smoke? I pulled my hoodie sleeves down over my arms.

Well, jeez, why'd I ever leave? Oh, right...my parents split up and moved, I had a full scholarship, and the whole Adrien fiasco didn't help much. Fucking Adrien Daniel O'Rourke. *Aydo.* My nickname for him since it was short for his first name, but also his initials, A.D.O. It figured as soon as I set foot back in this place, nostalgia pounced on me like a hungry lion.

Our crew was putting on a show tonight at the ballroom, along with a few other musical acts and some deejay I'd never heard of.

Hah! They finally unlocked the doors for us!

"Vava, let's go! Let's go!" I nudged Nova with my hip to move inside the blissfully air-conditioned building. I swear, if I have a sunburn...

The stage manager gave us a quick tour--I didn't utter a word that I knew this building intimately from *before*--and showed us to the dressing area. We had only two hours until show time and our makeup wasn't going to do itself!

* * *

The lights came down and we were finished with another satisfying performance. We slipped back stage, pulled on our cover-ups and made our way out into the main area to mingle. Years ago, when Nova and I first started our duo, we pinky-promised we would always make time for audience members after a show...someday when we were famous. Though we're *not* famous by most standards, the people that come to support our art deserve our appreciation--if only for five or ten minutes. Being kind like that gets you remembered...and gets more followers on your Twitter feed and likes on your Facebook page. Wink, wink, nudge, nudge.

The headlining band ripped out their opening song and it was already getting loud, but there were a few patrons hovering around the bar area that seemed to be waiting on our motley group of gypsies.

As I finished being hugged-a-bit-too-long by one fan and took a quick selfie with another, I looked down to stretch the back of my neck--metal headdresses are heavy, people--and a shadow fell over my bare toes.

When I looked up, I felt the blood drain from my face. Surely, I was seeing an apparition. A six-three, black-haired, green-eyed apparition. I couldn't blink and I couldn't speak.

Nova elbowed me, before turning to *him* to introduce herself. "Hi, there. Did you enjoy the show?"

Fucking Adrien.

He was jarred out of his own trance and politely extended his hand to my friend, "Hi, I'm Adrien. Yes, I really did enjoy it--I've never seen anything like it."

I still stared in shock, but came out of it when Nova cleared her throat and nudged me again.

Naturally, my filter chose that moment to stop working, so instead of a civil greeting out came, "What the *fuck* are *you* doing here?!" Aaand I was all up in his space.

He raised his hands, palms toward me in an unspoken entreaty, "Luce, I just had to see if it was really you."

I poked him in the chest, "Don't call me that! It's Stella now."

He flinched when I jabbed him and his voice was soft, "I had hoped you would have a few minutes to speak with me."

If it were possible, my eyes widened even more. As I took a deep breath to verbally flay him alive, Nova's hand on my shoulder stopped me. When I looked over at her she gave a subtle shake of her head. Nova was my best friend and just about the only person on earth I actually listened to. So, I relented.

"I'll grab our stuff and see you back at the hotel." Just like that, my buffer was gone.

I looked down and focused on my feet as I took several deep, grounding breaths, letting my jaw relax and my fists unclench. When I straightened my posture and met his eyes again, I was calm and icily cool. On the outside at least. My anger was aimed where it needed to be: at myself. I couldn't understand the urge I was feeling to jump into his arms.

Keeping my tone neutral, I said, "Let's go have a drink." I didn't wait for him to answer or follow as I headed straight for an empty stool at the bar.

I slapped the counter, "Gin and tonic, for the love of the gods!" The bartender smirked and nodded as he turned to make my liquid courage.

Adrien had, in fact, followed me and now sat on my left. I sighed, "So, what is it you wanted to discuss?"

He smirked and I ignored the little jump I felt in my stomach at the familiar expression, "Still direct, Lu-*Stella*," he amended quickly at the snap of my glare.

"And you are apparently still using the same dark, cryptic and mysterious bullshit." I took a long swig of my drink. *Oh, gin, you never let me down.*

I couldn't help but thaw--marginally, of course--when he slumped, elbows on the bar top, with his hands covering his face. Allowing myself a moment of weakness, I took the opportunity to study his long, artist's fingers, noting how much more weathered and callused they were compared to the way I remembered them. Hard work and countless hours playing guitar had shaped those hands. A memory floated to the forefront of my mind of those same fingers stroking delicately down my throat, sternum and waist so many times. Even now, I had goose bumps.

Adrien's voice broke my reverie, "You used to look at me that way all the time."

In that moment I was thankful for the heavy stage makeup that concealed my blushing face.

"I wasn't looking *at* you. I was thinking. Thinking about....*Oscar.* My...*boyfriend.*" *Really? That's the best you could come up with?!*

It appeared that Adrien believed me, however, because his face fell a little at my lie. "Oh...I see."

I sighed and rubbed my temples. "Look, Adrien. I apologize for being hostile earlier, but I am *longing* for you to say your piece so that I can limp back to my hotel room and crash." I took a risk and laid my hand on his exposed forearm that still rested on the bar.

Oh, that was a bad idea...

Electricity zinged between us and it felt just like before, years ago. We were Aydo and Luce again. When I tried to jerk my hand away, Adrien stopped me. My breath stuttered in my lungs at the feel of his thumb stroking the inside of my wrist. In a slight panic, I looked around the room with the hope that Nova was still lurking there somewhere. The traitor was nowhere to be found.

"Lu--Stella, *please.* I came home to visit my parents before I go back on tour with my band, *Loft*. I saw you on the poster for the Ballroom and I thought I had gone mad. In seven years, you have never been far from my thoughts. *Never.* You've been my constant muse and I thought I would never see you again. I've been looking for you, Luce; I've been looking for you ever since you left me." The last was spoken in a whisper.

I felt a shiver from my scalp all the way down to my ankles at this fervent confession. Instead of addressing it, however, I said, "You keep calling me Luce, Aydo."

"That's because that's who you are to me. And it's not like it's a big stretch from your real name, *Lustella*." That smirk again.

"It's the dumbest name ever! Shhh!" I covered his mouth with my free hand. Another mistake I quickly realized when the silky texture of his lips sent a current of desire straight to my lady bits. I whipped it away and grabbed up my drink again to prevent Adrien from any further hand-trapping.

He didn't miss that mini-meltdown, but chose to be a gentleman and ignore it.

"Luce, I know I fucked up with you. So very badly. I overheard someone say that you always come out to mingle after shows, so I stuck around. If this was my one and only second chance, I didn't want to miss it."

How did we ending up sitting so close? I observed my knees nestled between his, our torsos leaning towards each other...I was woefully out of control in this situation. He had done it again!

"Aydo..." I watched his eyes glow at my special nickname for him.

"I didn't know where you had gone and no one else did either!"

I laughed lightly, "Well, you know that I have no relatives in this state. I changed my name when I moved with my dad and started college in Washington."

His head dropped as he shook it in disbelief, "You've been on the west coast the *whole time*?"

I finally freed my captured wrist and crossed my arms protectively over my chest, "Yes, well, I live in Portland now, but...what about it?"

He shoved agitated fingers through his thick mane of ebony waves, "It's just that I've been living in California. You were close to me and I had no idea."

"Adrien, I don't see why that matters. We were done. I moved away and that was the end of it."

He took hold of my hands again, "Did you miss the part where I said I've been looking for you for the last seven years? I wanted to apologize, take it all back...tell you the truth of how I really felt."

All at once it was too much for me, and I stood up so fast my stool nearly fell over. Ripping my hands away, I said, "Enough. I'm exhausted and I can't hear this right now. You shouldn't have come here." As I fled the building, I motioned for one of the bouncers to prevent Adrien from following me.

2

"Well?" Nova queried as soon as I shut the door of our shared suite.

I held up my hand, "Just let me get changed and showered first, okay?" I barely recognized my own voice with the decidedly defeated tone in it.

"Okay, whenever you're ready." Nova was good at not pushing, though I could feel the vibration of her curiosity from across the room.

Thirty minutes later, I sat on the edge of her bed, carefully combing out my wet, hip-length hair.

"So--" she began and I tensed, "that's THE Adrien?"

I sighed, rotating my head to stretch my neck, "Yes. He has apparently been looking for me since I left and thought that Fate had granted him a gift. He felt he should seize the moment and try to...to...win me back? Make amends? I have no idea what he thinks to accomplish. It's too weird for me to even process, and it's been too long. I told you how it went...My parents divorced that year and went their separate ways. I changed my name and didn't really *want* to be found by anyone. For the average person, finding me would have been near impossible."

"Back that up...*win you back*?" Nova sat up.

"He didn't say that in so many words, but he was all 'this is my second chance, I had to take it' blah-blah-blah..." I stood again and walked back to the bathroom to deposit my comb. When I came back and slid under the covers of my own bed, I laid on my side, facing Nova.

She had this excited expression on her face, to which I quirked a brow, "Down, girl. He's most certainly just trying to get into my panties." I didn't sound particularly convincing to myself, so I knew I wasn't fooling my bestie.

"Come on, Stel, who do you thinking you're fooling?"

I sighed heavily and rolled to my back, fixing my gaze on the ceiling, "Honest, or not, it's still too late and far, far too bizarre. I'm just glad we're leaving tomorrow and it is good riddance once again."

I set the alarm on my phone, "Love you Vava. 'Night."

"Luhyounightnight!" Nova switched off the lamp and settled in.

My sleep was, thankfully, dreamless.

3

"Holy...forty-seven more likes and twenty-two follows since last night!" Nova announced from her seat as we got settled on the plane.

"Awesome." I replied absently, my eyes closed.

"Uh...Stel?"

I rolled my head towards her and opened my eyes.

She glanced from me, to her tablet and back to me again a few times before dramatically exhaling and handing it to me.

"What is it?" I smiled as I took it from her and looked down at the screen.

"Sonofabitch."

Not only had Adrien found the *Candéo* Facebook and Twitter, he'd uploaded and tagged me in a bunch of old photos. Oh, great...he'd posted song lyrics from his band's new album. Apparently, they were about yours truly.

Worse? Our fans were eating. It. Up. *Turncoats*, I thought bitterly.

I tried to calm and center myself, I really did. I was marginally successful as I enlarged and looked through the pictures I had been tagged in. I knew his game...he wanted me to feel nostalgic, feel all gooey and remember the good times we had.

Most of the images were candid shots from the many plays we were in together, but there were others that were more intimate. His arrow had hit the mark.

Our first outing with our mixed group of friends was a bonfire out by a lake. I vaguely remember someone snapping random pictures that night, including the one I looked at now.

* * *

I couldn't hide my trembling hands and knees. Adrien made me so nervous and he smelled so good I couldn't control myself.

We'd only spent time together at school, voice lessons and during shows up until now, except for our first date last week. He hadn't tried to kiss me then, so I wondered when it would happen.

One of his friends, Kyle, had busted out his guitar and was playing softly on the other side of the fire from us. It was a surprisingly chilly, late summer evening and Adrien had his arm around me to ward off the cold.

I startled when I realized that as I had been tacitly observing all of his friends and my friends interacting with each other, Adrien had been observing me.

"What?" I smiled at him.

He shook his head, "Nothing. You just look gorgeous by firelight."

I rolled my eyes and bumped my shoulder against his chest, "Nice one."

He lifted his hand and tucked a wayward strand of hair behind my ear, "I'm serious, Luce. You look amazing. I wish we weren't with all of these people right now."

"Oh, really? What would you be doing then?" I was a little shocked by my own boldness.

Adrien stared into my eyes and I stared right back. Slowly, so slowly, we moved into each other and brushed our lips together. My skin hummed and tingled all over as he lit me up with his mouth.

* * *

I felt that same tingle looking at the photo that captured the moment right before our lips touched, our eyes locked and the bonfire raging in front of us. That was the night I had really started to fall for him.

The next few images were of us singing together. That was actually how we had first met. To hear him tell it, he showed up early for his voice lesson one day and heard the voice of an angel. Intrigued, he poked his head around the corner to see who possessed such a voice and was struck dumb when he saw me standing there. We busted him immediately, of course.

Lisette was our teacher and introduced us. The rest of course, was history. Lisette, being the meddlesome person she was, took it upon herself to insist we work on some songs *together*. With or without our being in a relationship, his velvety baritone blended perfectly with my own mezzo soprano.

He'd begun dabbling with guitar and piano already, so we did some open mic nights together in addition to the classical pieces we worked on with Lisette.

My breath hitched when the screen showed a photo of us from a wedding gig. We had performed "Come What May" from *Moulin Rouge* and in this shot, we stood facing one another, Aydo's hand on my cheek.

I looked up, reflecting about the look on his face from that night and realized I was smiling.

Rat bastard! I forced my face into a scowl.

There were many, many more. Picture after picture of us kissing, laughing, and smiling—I paused when I saw one I didn't remember at all. It was of Adrien looking at me without my knowledge. The soft expression on his face...I didn't remember the final image either. I remember the day it was taken, but I didn't know anyone had been shooting pictures that day.

It was right after holiday break and we had both traveled to different places. I hadn't seen him in over a week and as I walked across the courtyard at school I heard him shouting my name. It was all very movie-like as we ran to each other, I jumped into his arms and he swung me around. There was a look of utter and complete joy on Adrien's face that I remember seeing more often than I could count while we were together. He looked so replete.

So, there I was stuck in my memories and naturally the old issues rose to the surface. I felt pissed off again, because I knew back then that Aydo's feelings for me had been more than what he said out loud. But having this visual proof didn't do anything to alter the fact that he had obliterated me. I had been at a fragile point in my life when we were together and he exploited it.

"What's the saying? 'You always hurt the one you love'?" I muttered to no one in particular.

I located *Loft's* Facebook page and looked around, noting with no little amount of horror that their first tour stop was New Orleans...as in where Nova and I were headed right now.

"Sonofabitch."

"You said that already." Nova grabbed her tablet back from me when the flight attendant shot us a dirty look.

"Well, I meant it. Both times!" I whispered fiercely.

She slugged me in the arm, "Don't you yell at me!" Her voice was the same hushed volume as mine.

We stared each other down, wearing twin expressions not unlike an angry pug, but the standoff quickly dissolved into giggles.

"Shithead," She said affectionately.

"Twat waffle." I replied.

"Nice!" We fist bumped and started giggling again.

* * *

In the air, Nova asked, "So—what are you going to do? He's stirring up a lot of drama—at least on the interwebs."

I dropped my head back against my seat and closed my eyes again, "He certainly is. I really don't know what to do. It seems ridiculous to me to humor him. I can't accept the idea of him pining all this time. And I've loved others since the Epic-ness that was Aydo and Luce..." *loved* might be a stretch. Briefly infatuated? Much more apt.

I stroked an imaginary beard while I pondered all of this seriousness.

"Well, I guess we'll wait and see what happens in New Orleans...don't think I didn't notice what it said on *Loft's* page!" Nova bumped her shoulder against mine and I grunted.

We'll see, indeed...

4

When we landed in New Orleans, I turned on my phone only to be bombarded with an inordinate amount of missed calls, voice mails, text messages, and push notifications.

"Jeez!" I hurriedly turned the ringer off—which Nova had brilliantly changed to a loud, juicy fart noise without my knowledge. You could imagine the looks I received when it started going off.

I skimmed through, seeing a bunch of the same comments and likes that I had seen earlier when I was using Nova's tablet.

Fuck. There were two missed calls and more than a dozen text messages from the same, unknown number. Except that I *did* know it. Aydo hadn't changed his cell since high school.

I guess if anyone was going to abuse the public information of Facebook and gank my phone number, it would be Adrien. Most people don't even pay attention to that stuff, but the savvy few used it to their advantage. Apparently, Adrien fit into that category like I did.

I scrolled to the bottom and began reading his messages in chronological order.

-This is your number isn't it?

-I know it is; you would want that type of control.

Well, fuck you very much! I thought acidly.

-Okay, Luce, clearly you don't recognize my number anymore even though I never changed it.

-Are you on a plane?

-Must be. OK. You'll just have a slew of messages when you turn your phone back on. I already left two voicemails.

-We took an earlier flight. I'm already in New Orleans.

-Look, I'm sorry I ambushed you last night. I should have known better.

-Don't be mad about the Facebook and Twitter stuff. If you look deeper, which I know you will, you'll see that all of those pictures have been on there for a long time. I only just tagged you in them now, because I finally found you. So there.

I *did* take a minute to look deeper, because he couldn't lie about when he posted things. Sure enough, most of the photos had been uploaded three or more years ago. The album was labeled 'My Muse'.

I couldn't help but snort and roll my eyes.

I was thankful for Nova then, as I had been walking and looking at my phone with my free arm hooked through hers. I knew I could rely on her to get me safely to the baggage claim.

I dimly hoped that she hadn't been talking to me though, because I had been utterly preoccupied.

5

Another fucking hot state. I loved Louisiana, but I don't know what possessed me to agree to come here in the middle of the summer.

"Vava, I'm melting!" I whined as we made our way out of the airport and joined our group by the rental van.

"How you think *I* feel, Stel?" She panted, "My people come from friggin' Sweden—I don't cope with this shit." Her fair face was splotchy from the smoldering blast of humid air.

We had only done a single night in Tulsa, but we were in New Orleans for three days. *Oh, joy and rapture.* My skin was going to be seared from my body if we didn't get in the van, crank the air conditioning, and vamoose.

I should have known my escape wouldn't be that simple.

"Luce!" an instant knot of tension formed at the base of my skull. I turned to see Aydo jogging towards me looking completely unaffected by the oppressive Big Easy air. *Ass.*

"Adrien, so nice to see you," I bit out.

"Did you get my messages?" He leaned against the van, shading me from the sun with his height. *Well, that was nice of him...*

"Of the hundred and ninety-four that you sent?" I quirked a brow with a half-smile.

"Touché." He had the nerve to look bashful and my fingers twitched as a lock of glossy, raven hair fell across his forehead. I remembered all too well how silky those strands felt against my palms as I used them to anchor his mouth to mine. I felt hot all over and in this case I couldn't blame the sultry, southern climate.

"We have to get going to our hotel, but...Um, I'll talk to you later, okay?" What the hell was I saying? His smoky jade eyes lit up and he grinned, showing his perfectly even, white teeth. I licked those once. *Damn it!* I shook my head at that creeper of a mind-trail.

"We're playing at La Pétite Théatre tomorrow night." I had started to move towards the van's door, but abruptly halted.

"You're kidding, right? That's where *we* are performing."

Aydo put his hands up in surrender, "I had nothing to do with the booking, Luce. This tour has been arranged for several months."

I glared at him.

He crossed his heart, "Honest! Don't use those blue laser beams on me, you know I'm powerless against them."

I snorted, "Okay, well...I guess I'll see you tomorrow night then."

His head drooped, "Oh, I guess that's still later...See you then." He spun on his heel and shuffled off toward his band mates. I recognized Kyle as one of the members—Kyle from our high school bonfire days. He waved at me, smiling. I lifted my chin in acknowledgement, then boarded the van and plopped down next to Nova. She'd disappeared on me when Adrien showed up. Sneaky wench.

Her smile was smug.

I frowned at her, "Oh, stop it, you."

She didn't say anything more, just chuckled at my discomfort.

* * *

All hotels pretty much looked the same when you travel as much as we do, and this three-star edifice on the edge of the French Quarter was not any different.

Our group all had rooms on the same floor, Nova and I being in our usual two-queen suite.

I didn't really care where we stayed, as long as the room was spotless and there was a mountain of pillows that varied in levels of firmness for me to collapse upon.

Nova set her bags on the bed nearest the window and flopped onto the mattress with a heavy sigh.

"I'm not used to being this tired," she said quietly.

I answered on a yawn, "Ditto. I think I might just take a nap right now, we don't have any obligations tonight."

My phone chose that moment to begin farting.

I covered my face with a pillow and screamed before glancing at the caller ID.

Oh, it's just my dad.

"Daddy, hi! How are my babies?" I got up and went to sit in the hallway. My dad was house-sitting for me and taking care of my cat and dog.

"Hey, kiddo. Mata and Edgar are fine. I just got back from a jog with Edgar and Mata is curled up in the window. " I could picture him sitting in his favorite leather recliner in my living room, still handsome and fit in his sixties with silver hair and the periwinkle eyes I had inherited.

"Aw, I'm glad they're okay. Thanks again for staying with them; I know it must be inconvenient."

"It's my pleasure, honey. I don't mind one bit. Your step-mother is getting all sorts of redecorating ideas for our place since we've been here." He chuckled, "Enough about me, though. How's my superstar?"

"Tired, but good. Tickets are still continuing to sell out at every venue, so we can't complain." *Don't say anything about Adrien...*

"You sound a little off. Are you sure everything is okay?" *Damn.* The old man's perceptiveness hadn't diminished one bit.

"Yeah, I mean...just hit a bit of a bump in Tulsa, but I'm handling it." I began to chew the inside of my cheek.

"Do you want to talk about it?" The chair creaked. He must be sitting forward.

I banged the back of my head lightly against the wall, "Promise you won't flip?"

"Depends, *Lustella Angelica,*" Uh oh...my full name.

"I sort of...ran into Adrien." I rushed the last part, but his hearing was still sharp, too.

"WHAT?!" I held the phone away as his deep voice roared through my tiny phone speaker.

My father *hated* Adrien for what he did. I shuddered as I remembered the innumerable, awful things he'd threatened to do to him for me.

"I said I'm handling it. Anyway, that was a long time ago, you shouldn't be so angry anymore, Daddy." I crossed my fingers as I said these words, knowing full well that *I* was not practicing what I was preaching.

He sat in silence on the other end.

"Daddy?"

"I'm sorry, you're—you're right. It's just that I remember how you cried yourself to sleep for weeks after he broke things off, and how he acted around you with those other girls. It was almost like he was trying to convince you he wasn't any good."

Ding! The proverbial light bulb went off above my head. "Dad, I think you just answered the question that has bothered me all these years. You're a genius!"

His laughter rumbled over the line, "I don't know about all that, but I'm glad you're okay. Still, if he tries anything...remember what I taught you, okay? I love you."

"I love you, too. Talk to you soon; please tell Alice I said hi and give my babies a scratch for me."

After he hung up, I remained in the hallway with my memories.

* * *

These girls won't stop giggling every time they walk by me, it's getting annoying.

"Hey, you two. What the hell do you keep giggling about? Do I have toilet paper stuck to my shoe or something?" They were short, so I straightened to my full five-foot-ten for added intimidation.

They shared a secret look before staring up at me with matching smirks. They were perky, blonde and what I would label as "mean girls".

"You're dating Adrien O'Rourke, right?" Mean Girl 1 asked.

"Yes, why?" I narrowed my eyes.

Mean Girl 2 stepped closer, I think trying to affect a conspiratorial air which just came off as invading my personal space with her tacky perfume.

"We were just wondering how long you were going to last before he pops your cherry then moves on. That's what he does, you know. You're still pretty new around here, so maybe you hadn't heard. You met over the summer, right?"

"Who the hell are you people, the CIA?" I started to get anxious and sweaty, none of which I let show to these two pieces of work.

"We're just looking out for you. We girls have to stick together. Bye now." They turned in unison and sauntered off.

I leaned against my locker and closed my eyes, trying to calm down. I gasped and opened them again when a shadow fell over me.

"Oh, Adrien." I forced a smile for him, because I didn't want to get into any sort of fight or uncomfortable conversation with him right now.

"Were you expecting someone else? Come here," He slipped his arms around my waist, dipping his head to capture my lips.

Mean Girl 1 and 2 disappeared from my mind, along with any doubts they tried to plant, as I let the current of tingles take over. I sighed and lightly bit Adrien's bottom lip, making him groan and press me against the wall.

He pulled back to look down into my face. He wore an expression I was seeing on him more and more lately, a light shining in his eyes and a breathless wonder.

"You better get to class, Luce. My Bronco is in the shop, can I catch a ride with you today?"

I nodded and gently set my teeth on his chin making him laugh and squeeze me tight.

"Later, Aydo."

*He brushed a kiss on my nose before I headed off to class, glancing over my shoulder a few times to find Adrien watching me, **that** look on his face once again.*

The thought crossed my mind, not for the first time, that Adrien was almost too good to be true.

6

The next day I stood on the edge of the stage at La Pétite Théatre, shielding my eyes from the lights as I shouted at the guy running sound, "Can we get just a tad more volume and lower the bass a bit?"

I saw him give a thumbs-up from the booth and backed up to center stage next to Nova as we did a light run-through of our set for the coming evening.

Spin, lock, undulate up, and undulate down. We had this, but when you know a piece inside and out it is actually easier to make mistakes.

Fifteen minutes later, we moved aside to let the rest of our people run through their pieces. It would be another hour or so until we could join everyone for the group finale.

I heard a slow, deliberate clap from the back of the house and as I peered out, I realized Adrien and the rest of *Loft* were watching our rehearsal.

Nova elbowed me, "Go say hi,"

"You're not the boss of me," I griped.

"No, but I know all your passwords..." She menaced playfully.

"Fair enough." I hopped off the edge of the stage and strolled to the back to see the boys. And Adrien.

Kyle stood and opened his arms, "Luce! It's been forever! What are the odds, huh?"

I gave him an affectionate hug, "Hey, bud. Good to see you, how have you been?" He still had the boyish, ruddy-cheeked face I remembered, but the slightly chubby football player was no more. He was well-muscled and sported a tousled, blond surfer 'do.

"Living the dream, Luce." Kyle had always been gregarious and I was happy to see that hadn't changed as he kept his arm around me in a brotherly fashion.

I caught Adrien's frowning face and realized he didn't see Kyle touching me as 'brotherly'. Making sure no one else was looking, I stuck my tongue out at him in a completely mature and polished manner. He raised both eyebrows in surprise, then grinned as he shook off whatever mood he'd been in.

Kyle introduced me to the rest of the group and I sat down to visit for a bit.

Adrien was the lead vocalist, *of course*, but Kyle actually played lead guitar while Adrien played second. They switched off depending on the song, but that was the way they did it most of the time. Kyle's skills must have improved by leaps and bounds since the last I had heard them.

"Luce, you and the rest of your crew should hang with us after the show tonight." This was from Kyle.

"Yeah, that sounds good. We're catching a red eye out of Louis Armstrong tomorrow night, so we can stay up as late as we want." I glanced over my shoulder to check the progress of the drum solo that was happening right behind me. It was almost time for me to go back up.

Adrien had remained silent the whole time I sat with his band, instead choosing to watch me interact and catch up with Kyle and make fast friends with their drummer, Toko. He had more ink than I did and it was done in a beautiful and vibrant traditional Japanese style that filled me with envy.

I finally made eye contact and stared Adrien down for a moment.

He blinked and shifted in his chair, "What?"

"You tell me. You've been studying me for the last forty minutes without speaking." I was sitting backwards and resting my chin on my crossed arms I had draped over the back of the seat.

His smile was soft, "Honestly? This all feels very surreal to me, having you here. But, it also kind of feels like the old days...we're just a little older and with new people. I'm a bit overwhelmed."

I decided to be real for a moment, too, instead of defensive, "I know what you mean. It's like a blending of two worlds."

"Do you think we'll be able to find some time to talk? I haven't checked your tour schedule again, so I don't know if our paths are going to intersect after this." He sat forward, elbows on his knees.

I glanced down at his arms and noticed something new. "Hey, when did you get that?"

He followed my gaze to his right forearm where a tattoo of a nightingale rested. It was beautifully done with fine details and finished in a soft color-wash so it looked like an old-school birdwatcher's book drawing.

"I got it about five years ago when *Loft* recorded its first E.P." He ran his hand over the design.

"Is that...is that what I think it is?" My throat was closing up as a lump of emotion settled there.

He didn't reply, but he didn't need to. His eyes held the answer.

* * *

Moonlight picnics. Now that we were both eighteen, we could stay out past curfew without a care. Our favorite spot was the playground down the street from my house.

After dining on a gourmet selection of sparkling grape juice, potato chips and onion dip, we laid side by side on a blanket looking up at the stars and the full, bright moon.

"Aydo," I whispered, "do you hear that?" There was a faint but lively tune on the wind coming from a nearby tree.

He rose up on his elbows to listen more closely. "Is that a nightingale?"

"I think so." I replied, still listening.

He lay back down, his head so close that our hair mingled.

"That's you, Luce. My nightingale...my songbird. I could barely write my own name before you, and now the lyrics never stop." He linked his pinky with mine as the little bird continued to serenade us.

I was glad he wasn't looking at me, or else he would see the silent tears drifting from my eyes. His ardent words had affected me so deeply. Every time he spoke, he always managed to move me in some way and every time he moved me, I fell in deeper.

I covertly wiped away any evidence of my emotions, and then turned my head to press a kiss to his temple. "You're ridiculous, Aydo."

He rolled onto his side, gazing down at me, "It's your fault I'm this way. My street cred? Ruined." He lowered his lips to mine in a gentle caress.

He started to raise his head from me, but I had other plans. I slid my fingers into his hair and pulled him back, trapping his fuller bottom lip with my teeth.

He chuckled and murmured against my mouth, "My little songbird is feisty this evening...could it be the full moon?" Then he plundered me with his tongue, savoring and tasting me as he ran his fingertips down the side of my neck, across my collarbone, my breastbone, over my sensitive ribcage until he finally stopped at my hip, gripping me tight as he continued to stroke my tongue with his own.

* * *

I gasped when I felt those very fingers patting me on the arm.

"What!?" My face was burning up.

"Where'd you go on me, Luce?" Adrien's soft black eyebrows were arched in concern.

I sucked my cheeks in and bit down before responding, "I'm just...tired. I must have spaced out, I'm sorry."

"My tattoo *is* a nightingale." He said quietly.

I could only nod, suddenly grateful that Nova chose that moment to whistle at me: my cue to return to the stage for a group run-through. I hoped he didn't notice my shaking knees as I made my way back. Nonetheless, I felt a warm trail running down my body as I walked away and I glanced back to bust him watching me.

I couldn't stop my grin after that.

* * *

There was a soft knock on the dressing room door and one of the drummers, Ethan, answered it. He spoke quietly to the person on the other side before calling me over.

I had just placed my other strip of eyelashes on my lid as I stood and padded to the door, waving my hands at my face to speed up the glue-drying process.

"Thanks, Ethan," He was a quiet, eccentric young man that didn't say much and so I wasn't bothered by his non-verbal nod as he made his way back to his wife, Selene.

I peered through the opening, unsurprised to find Adrien standing there, hands in his jeans pockets, shifting nervously in his Converse sneakers.

"Hey," I stepped into the hallway and leaned back against the dressing room door.

He did a double take when he looked at me, his jaw going slack.

I felt a bit smug, knowing full well how I looked in full costume and makeup. My headdress wasn't on yet, so my mahogany hair cascaded in mermaid waves over my shoulders and all the way to my hips. My cheekbones were highlighted in iridescent glitter and my full lips were painted an alluring plummy red.

With fake eyelashes, my deep set blue eyes looked impossibly large.

"Close your mouth, darling." I affected a flawless British accent.

"Sorry, I just...I mean I saw you like this the other night, but it was dark. You look...you...*damn*. You're a fucking goddess." As if he couldn't stop himself, he moved towards me so I had to tilt my head back to look at him.

His scent assailed me and I felt an instant tightening in my lower belly and...*lower*. He smelled like cloves and whatever his natural chemistry was throwing out to entice my olfactory senses. I broke out in goose bumps, my nipples hardening underneath the thick fabric of my dance bra.

He just stood there, breathing my air. I knew the moment he caught my scent when his green irises disappeared as his pupils dilated.

I couldn't help it, really. The reactions of my own body were completely biological! When he stepped into me, I lost it.

Adrien lifted his hand and grazed his fingers down the side of my face to my neck where he paused, brushing his thumb over my stuttering pulse. He stared at that spot before lifting his gaze to mine, a question laid bare to me.

My vocal chords were paralyzed, so I slid my palms over his abs and chest, burying my fingers in his hair.

He bent his head towards me, stopping when just our noses brushed. "I'm going to mess up that lipstick."

I found my voice long enough to say, "Fuck my lipstick."

Then he claimed me.

Adrien pressed me into the steel door, one hand still cupping the back of my neck while the other gripped me behind the knee, lifting it so I could wrap my leg around his hips. I felt the hard ridge of him rub against my center and I moaned into his mouth, tugging his bottom lip with my teeth.

"God, I've missed that," Adrien whispered into me, coaxing and seducing my tongue with his.

I was burning up. I couldn't believe our chemistry still blazed like this after so many years apart. My pelvis tilted into him instinctively and my clit throbbed when I felt him swell even larger beneath the tight confines of his jeans.

The sound of the doorknob turning was like an ice bath and we sprung apart, clinging to opposite sides of the hallway, our chests heaving. There was no way to hide what we'd been doing, since my lipstick was smeared all over his face and mine.

Nova poked her head around the door, her blue-grey eyes widening in surprise, "Hi, guys...um, Stel, we need to finish up and...um, you should probably reapply your lip color. Adrien, good to see you..." Her cheeks flamed as she closed the door again.

I pulled a tissue from the pocket of my cover up and crossed to Adrien to clean him up, "Let me fix you."

He watched my face as I removed all traces of our make out session and when I tried to move away, he held my hands at the wrists against his chest.

"Luce, are you okay?"

I closed my eyes and breathed him in before looking up, "I think so. I'm still pretty confused about everything and you're by no means off the hook."

His eyes lit and crinkled at the corners with his smile, "I know. I shouldn't be. But, that was..."

"Yeah, it was."

"I'll see you after the show," He pulled me in, kissing the part in my hair before releasing me.

I'm in so much trouble, I thought to myself as I escaped to the dressing room to fix my face and finish getting ready.

7

"Hey there, New Orleans, how are we doing tonight?"

Oh, damn. I forgot what Adrien was like on stage. He was always charismatic and charming, but up there it was magnified to the nth degree.

The crowd at the theatre had thus far been a great audience and had really seemed to enjoy the belly dancers and musicians from our set. I was at the back of the house still chatting with a few appreciative spectators as Adrien and Kyle strummed the opening bars of their first song of the evening. The women in attendance were crowding around the front of the stage and calling out flirtatious and suggestive remarks.

Nova and I settled in at a table of our own, a waitress appearing magically to take our drink orders.

"Mineral water, please." Vava wasn't a teetotaler; she'd just never imbibed in her life and didn't think it prudent to start now.

"Hmmm...how about a dirty gin martini with extra olives?" I was feeling fancy this evening.

As the waitress left to get our beverages, Nova zeroed in on me. I glanced at her out of the corner of my eye, "What?"

"Don't you 'what' me, Stella. You made out with Adrien!" She poked me in the ribs making me yelp.

I slapped her hand away, "Yes, I did. He…he still affects me. I don't understand it, but he does."

"So, what now?" she asked, sipping the water our waitress plunked down in front of her along with my martini.

I took a long sip before answering, "I really don't know, Vava. I thought I had moved past this, but as soon as I saw him in Tulsa…" I shook my head.

She reached out and squeezed my hand, "Do you want my opinion?"

"Always."

"I think you should hear him out. They were the actions of an 18-year-old boy, Stel. Up there on that stage right now? That's a man. A man who looks at you like it is Christmas morning. The only times I see you lit up like this is when we're performing. You're really awake now, Stel. You trust my gut, right?"

I nodded, "Second only to my own."

"Then you know you agree with me."

I inhaled deeply and let it release, "Yes."

We shared a long look of understanding, words no longer necessary.

That's when the subject of our conversation chose that moment to interrupt us.

"Luce, are you out there?" Adrien shielded his eyes as he peered out into the audience.

Nova nudged my chair with her foot, "Stand up!"

I took a hurried gulp of my drink and stood, giving a little wave.

"Guys, can we give another round of applause for this woman? She danced so beautifully this evening and I, for one, would love to have her join us up here. What do you say?" He held them under his spell and they cheered.

He grinned, "Come on, Luce!"

Performer that I am, I could never let down a crowd. I slipped *off* my kimono cover up and draped it over my chair as I slipped *on* my dance persona and made my way to the front of the house and Adrien's proffered hand.

As gracefully as possible, I climbed up next to him, much to the disappointment of the female audience members.

Through my smiling teeth, I asked, "What are you doing, Aydo?"

"You'll see." He lifted my fingers to his lips, his eyes skating down to my wrist before coming back up to burn into mine, "A green gardenia?"

I looked away, embarrassed.

He laughed, "Oh, this is going to be perfect."

Kyle starting picking out a melody that had me gasping, my eyes flying to him and then Adrien.

Adrien leaned in toward the microphone, watching me.

"Here, kid...look, I brought you flowers...green, red, blue....all things permanent and perfect for you, kid, you...I mean, all things...bright and beautiful... everything forever all...come...true...."

As if my feet had a mind of their own, I stepped up next to him; our gazes locked and I sang my verse.

"All things...bright and beautiful...everything forever...all...come...true..."

* * *

"I've got the perfect song for you two to work on." Lisette proclaimed as Adrien and I walked in for our joint lesson.

We had only spoken a few times over the last few weeks and this was the first time we would be working on something together. I was incredibly nervous, because I knew how good he was and I had never done a duet before.

He stood next to me by the piano, and every time he shifted, his arm would brush against me. I felt little prickles of awareness travel up my skin, raising the hairs along with my body temperature.

"This is called 'All Things Bright and Beautiful' and it's from **Marry Me a Little***." Lisette handed the sheet music to share, "Sorry, I only had one extra copy."*

I glanced up at her smirking face. Sure, she did.

After the lesson, Adrien walked me out to my car.

"So, what do you think?" He asked, leaning against the open door of my Pontiac.

"I like it...do you?" I was a bit nervous by his nearness. Adrien, I had quickly realized, had no concept for personal space...At least where I was concerned it seemed.

"I like it, too. But let me ask you this...have you ever seen a green flower?"

I frowned, thinking. "No, I can't say I have."

He lifted his chin, gazing at me speculatively.

"What?" I raised a hand to my face, checking for boogers or some other reason for his stare.

"Do you have markers by any chance?"

I blinked, confused by his reply. "Actually, I think so."
I gave him a light shove, startling at the electric
current that jumped between us, and opened the back
door of my car to pull out my backpack.

I dug around for a moment before producing a pack
of colorful permanent markers, which Adrien eagerly
snatched from me.

"Give me your wrist," He commanded.

I offered him my left arm and he immediately set to
work with the markers I provided.

When he finished, he smiled at me and I went
temporarily dumb. That boy had a smile that would
make a nun think twice about her lifestyle choices.

"Take a look," He urged.

When I regained my senses and looked at my wrist, I
was stunned. He had drawn a beautiful flower using
various shades of green.

"See? A green flower. It's a gardenia, which means
'you're lovely'...or sometimes it can symbolize a
secret love." He still held onto me and the skin
contact was distracting.

I swallowed nervously, "How about that. Thank you,
Aydo." I gently removed my arm from his hand and
beamed up at him.

His brow wrinkled slightly as he returned my grin,
"What did you call me?"

Shit, what did I say? Oh. *"Aydo. Short for Adrien and your initials...Adrien Daniel O'Rourke."*

Deliberately, he tucked a loose strand of hair behind my ear and I shivered, "Aydo. I love it. And you? You're Luce. Lustella is far too austere."

I nodded, "Okay, Luce it is."

Just then, Adrien's innate confidence failed him and he was suddenly shy, "Luce MacLean, would you...would you like to go out with me sometime?" He'd actually backed away, shoved his hands in his pockets and scuffed his shoes on the pavement of the driveway.

I bit my lower lip to curb my excitement before I calmly said, "Yes."

* * *

"And we'll be together tomorrow...and we'll be together on Monday....and we'll be together on April and Christmas and next year and always..." We finished in perfect harmony.

In the heat of the moment, Adrien locked his lips with mine in a searing kiss. The house erupted into loud, bawdy cheers and whistles as everyone got to their feet to give us a standing ovation.

"Luce, I love you." Adrien whispered.

I flinched away from him, stepping back to create distance.

"You did not just say that to me!" I hissed.

His face drained of color as he realized his misstep, not saying another word as I slid off the stage and hurried back to Nova at the back of the house.

"Hey, what's wrong?" Nova stood up to intercept me.

I grabbed my cover up and put it back on, wrapping it protectively around myself, "He just told me he loved me, Vava. What the hell?!"

I made a move towards the exit, but Nova stopped me.

"Stel, you need to calm the fuck down."

I closed my eyes and focused on my breathing, then turned back to our table to finish my martini. It was room temperature now, but the bite of the alcohol did the trick to ease my stress.

"Better?" She rubbed my upper arms.

I nodded.

"That was very impulsive of him, but not worth freaking out over, Stel. And by the way, *where* did you learn to sing like that? That was amazing!" She pulled me back down into our chairs and bounced excitedly.

I dimpled, "Thank you. Remember how I said Adrien and I met?"

Comprehension dawned, "Wow."

We remained there in the back and watched the rest of *Loft's* set.

I had two more martinis.

* * *

Loft and our gang stumbled into the hotel lobby, giggling.

"Funny how we're staying at the same hotel, eh, Luce?" Kyle remarked, slightly buzzed.

I was a little fuzzy, but still functional, "Yeah...these last few days have been one, big coincidence, Kyle..."

We made our way to the elevator and I punched number three at the same time Adrien did. We looked at each other, our fingers still on the button, and laughed.

"I give up!" I proclaimed, sinking against the wall until the door opened up on our floor.

Our group of dancers and musicians were all paired off in some way: close friends, siblings or significant others. The romantic partners were getting affectionate on the way to their rooms and I felt a slight pang as I thought about how long it had been for me since I'd...well, you know.

As we approached Nova's and my door, a familiar figure burst out into the hallway.

Nova shrieked with joy, "Honey!" It was her husband, Rhys.

Fuck, I thought. I forgot I had schemed with Rhys about this. It was their anniversary and he wanted to surprise her.

I felt my expression falter when I realized I had nowhere to sleep tonight. I hung back awkwardly as Adrien's group and mine shuffled toward their rooms.

Just before he went inside, Adrien turned, frowning when he saw my face. Hurrying back to me, he ducked his head to look in my eyes, "What's wrong?"

I grimaced as I spoke, "I...kinda forgot that Nova's husband was going to surprise her tonight and I failed to make alternate sleeping arrangements."

His eyes sparkled with mirth, "Well, the boys and I are in a two-bedroom suite with four beds and a pull-out couch. I can kick Kyle out of our room—I'm sure he wouldn't mind letting you have his bed for the night. I don't even think he's slept in it since we've been here."

"I can take the couch, Aydo. Are you sure you don't mind me interrupting guy time?" The warmth from his hands heated my skin through the material of my kimono.

"Grab your stuff and we'll get it sorted out, okay?" He brushed a light peck across my brow and pushed me gently towards my bedroom door where Rhys and Nova were still embracing.

"Hey, lovebirds, I'm going to grab my goodies and crash with *Loft* tonight." I squeezed past them and hurriedly snatched up my suitcase, makeup box and toiletries.

Nova tore her attention from Rhys for a moment, "Wait—are you sure?"

"Yes, I'm totally sure. I'll be right down the hall. You two have fun and I'll see you tomorrow. Happy anniversary." I gave them a wink and waggled my eyebrows before I stepped across the threshold where Adrien waited to take my bags.

8

"Hey, fellas. Sorry to crash on you tonight."

"No worries, Luce," Toko said from the kitchen before joining us in the living room.

"Seriously, take my empty bed. I have slept on this couch the whole time we've been here," this from Kyle who was reclining on said couch and flipping through channels on the flat screen.

"Here, follow me." Adrien schlepped my bags into the bedroom off to the left of where the boys were sprawled and watching TV.

"Hey, Luce?" Kyle's voice stopped me mid-turn.

"Yeah, bud?"

"Great having you sing with us tonight." He grinned sweetly at me and I had to go over to him and plop a kiss on his messy, blond head.

"Thanks, K. I had fun, too. I haven't performed in that way for a very long time." I ruffled his hair once more and trailed after Adrien.

There were two queen-sized beds—one of which appeared to still be pristine—and an en suite bathroom. I hadn't considered that even though I had a place to sleep, I wouldn't be alone in the room. Adrien would be in the bed right next to me. Maybe it was the martinis, our shared history, or both, but I wasn't bothered by the idea.

In a thoughtful move, Adrien laid my suitcase on what was now my bed, then carried my makeup box—it was a steel tool-box, actually—and my toiletry bag into the bathroom, setting them on the long vanity counter.

I hadn't moved from the doorway, simply choosing to watch him instead. When he stood before me, I stared at his chin.

Adrien lifted his hand towards my cheek, but halted, making a fist and letting it drop to his side, "I'll call housekeeping to bring some extra towels for you."

I nodded, shifting out of the way so he could pass and I closed the door behind him. Completely alone, the events of the day and evening washed over me and having no one to vent to, I did the only thing that I knew would help me decompress: self-grooming.

Shuffling into the bathroom, I began the long process of removing all of my jewelry, makeup and hair accoutrements.

Using the running sink as a cover, I let all of the emotions flood me and come out of my eyes, shaking and crying without a sound.

Once my face was scrubbed free of makeup, I felt a little less overwhelmed. My tears had cleansed me and, thankfully, the cold water from the sink prevented my eyes from being a red, puffy giveaway.

A light knock preceded Adrien's return with an obscene stack of fresh, fluffy towels.

"My lady," he bowed and presented them to me.

I chuckled, "There are at least twelve towels here, Aydo; were you planning on murdering me and needed extra for the clean-up?"

"You're a girl; I don't know how many towels girls need." His cheeks colored.

"Wow, I went from a lady to a girl in no time flat!" I biffed him in the face with one of the towels.

"Hey now! You know what I mean...stop hitting me!" He backed out of the bathroom, trying to escape my full-scale attack.

I laughed as I stalked him around the beds, brandishing the towel menacingly. I used his mattress as a springboard and tackled him on my bed, pummeling him lightly with the soft terrycloth.

"What has gotten into you?" He guffawed as I switched tactics to tickling his ribs. But he'd had enough and gripped my biceps, tugging me close to his face and pinning my hands between our chests. My hair had fallen forward and shrouded us in mahogany and purple-streaked waves.

"I don't know. You bring it out in me." I squirmed away and ran back to the bathroom, slamming it shut, "I'm showering now—don't come in."

His chuckle on the other side of the door turned sensual, "I'll give you to the count of ten and then I'm coming in."

My face flamed as I remembered him saying those very words to me before.

* * *

I had to change into something different. Adrien had announced we were going horseback riding, so my denim skirt wasn't going to cut it.

"I'm just going to go change into pants, okay?" I said this over my shoulder as I headed down the hallway to my bedroom.

I parted the beads in front of my door and closed it behind me, stripping out of my skirt and rummaging through my dresser for a pair of jeans. I squeaked when the beads rattled.

"Aydo! I will be out in a minute—don't come in!" I grabbed a stuffed animal from the floor and held it in front of me protectively.

"I'll give you until the count of ten—then, I'm coming in." His voice was dark.

The desire for him to come through that door—as I heard him begin to count—was almost overriding my virginal outrage as I turned and hurriedly found something to wear.

I shimmied into the snug denim—they must have just been washed—hopping around trying to ease my rounded bottom into them.

"Ten."

My eyes flew to the door, pants unfastened, as Adrien slowly opened it and pushed through the curtain of beads.

"Whatcha doing there?" His smile was positively wicked.

Desperation won out over embarrassment when I hopped in place and whined, "I can't zip them."

His lips twitched in amusement, eyes alight. "Do you need help, Luce?"

I gazed at him through narrowed eyes, "Yes, but no funny business."

Adrien moved towards me, reaching toward the waist of my jeans. His knuckles brushed against my lower belly and my muscles tightened instinctively.

He paused, glancing at my face, "Okay?"

I bit my lip and nodded.

He tracked the movement and swallowed hard before turning his attention back to my zipper. With a strong tug and a quick movement, I was secure.

"White lace thong, huh?" He bit the inside of his cheek.

I slapped him lightly on the arm, "Bad boy!"

"Have you met you, Luce?" He let his olive eyes roam all over me, heating me up from the inside out.

I gripped the collar of his white button-down shirt and dragged him to me for a kiss, sucking hard on his bottom lip making him growl and back me up until we tumbled onto my bed.

He was careful, as always, to never touch my breasts, bottom or...other place...when we made out and I was getting frustrated. When I would try to slide my hands down to his ass, he would move his hips away from me and distract me with a nibble or sweep of his tongue.

I groaned and turned my head away.

"What's wrong, little songbird?" He nuzzled the tender spot just under my ear and I shivered.

"It's just—look, I know you're not a virgin, okay? But, you never try anything with me, Aydo. You've never once copped a feel in the four months we've been together. Is there something wrong with me?" I hated sounding insecure, but really? I hadn't had sex yet, but I had certainly done more than this before.

Adrien looked down and laid his lips against my sternum, inhaling my scent.

"Luce, there's nothing wrong with you. You are absolutely perfect. Believe me, I want to do all manner of lewd and inappropriate things with you," I gasped when he actually let his hips lower against *me so I could feel that a special part of him was very interested in doing said inappropriate things.*

"So, what's stopping you?" I arched into him, eliciting a strangled sound from his throat.

"I want everything to be perfect with you. I have never felt this way before and I don't want to screw it up by taking things too far too soon." Not quite in control of himself, he punctuated this statement by rocking his pelvis into mine.

The friction was amazing and I felt a throbbing start to build.

"Luce, we have to go ride horses now." He extricated himself, longing on his face as he took me in, knees apart, shirt riding up showing my toned stomach. Without another word, he left my room.

"I'd rather ride you," I muttered.

* * *

When Adrien turned the knob and stepped into the bathroom, I hadn't taken off a single thing.

"Well, you're no fun." He pretended to pout.

I rolled my eyes, "Actually, I'm glad you're here. I need help."

"Oh, really?"

"Nova always ties my bra on for me and she double-knots it. Can you undo the knot for me?" I let the kimono drop to the floor, draping my hair over one shoulder and giving him my back. I watched him in the vanity mirror.

He gulped, his Adams apple jumping with nervousness.

"Please, Adrien? I really can't do it myself."

I saw how he took a deep breath and centered himself before coming near me as he started to work me free from the knotted ties of my bra.

It pleased me deep inside that I unsettled him this much and I felt very powerful—even though the brush of his knuckles on my back was sending little licks of heat straight to my center and I squeezed my thighs together, biting back a whimper.

"You're out." He spoke by my ear, his breath dancing over my skin.

"Thank you."

He left without another word.

I took a cold shower.

* * *

"Aydo," I poked my head out the bathroom door.

He was reclining on his bed and looked up at me from his phone, eyebrows arched in inquiry.

"There should be a pair of pajama pants and a *Candéo* tee right on top in my suitcase. Grab them for me, please?" I batted my eyelashes.

He rose and opened my shiny, purple suitcase, quickly finding what I asked for. His expression became calculating as he approached my towel-covered form.

"I don't trust that twinkle in your eye, Adrien O'Rourke." I tried to look stern, but I was secretly quivering in anticipation. He still quite literally made my knees weak.

"I was just thinking what a nice shirt this is and—oh, would you look at that—it's just my size..." He held the black unisex tee up in front of his torso, admiring the logo of Nova's and my face surrounded by bursts of starlight. It was true that I swam in that shirt, which was why I used it for sleeping...

"What are you getting at?" I quirked one perfectly-groomed brow.

"I propose a trade." Without a second thought, he dropped my clothes on the floor, stripped out of his *Loft* logo tee, and handed it to me before retrieving my pajama bottoms and handing those to me as well.

My mouth went dry at the sight of his lean, hard muscles wrapped in smooth, olive skin. He was built like a swimmer: broad through the chest and shoulders, then tapering down to the hips. But this was no longer the rangy boy I'd loved...present day Adrien was all man, as indicated by the light dusting of hair on his chest and happy trail. I could see the v-cut of his lower abs above the waist of his jeans and was nearly overwhelmed with the urge to bite him there. Then lick him. Repeatedly.

I gasped for air, realizing I had stopped breathing. Adrien wore a shit-eating grin, fully enjoying my lusty perusal.

"Had your fill?" He asked darkly.

I growled and slammed the door in his smug, beautifully-chiseled face.

He's trying to kill me.

I buried my face in his shirt and breathed in deeply. *Oh, gods...he is definitely trying to kill me.*

I slipped it on, luxuriating in the feel of the soft, organic cotton against my clean skin and slipped my satin sleep bottoms up over my hips. There is nothing better than smooth fabric against naked skin. Well, *almost* nothing better.

I tried to compose myself and returned to the bedroom, comb and hair-tie in hand.

Adrien was wearing my shirt and he very deliberately lifted the collar to scent it, staring at me with heat in his eyes.

"If you don't stop looking me like that, I'm either going to go share the couch with Kyle, or I'm going to jump you." My hands were on my hips in an effort to have some semblance of authority and self-control.

"Do I get to pick?" His excitement was childlike as he clapped his hands.

I moved my suitcase to the floor and sat cross-legged on my bed, facing Adrien. I frowned at him.

"I'm sorry, Luce. You drive me crazy with want...you always did." He ran frustrated hands over his face and through his hair, only making it sexier and more tousled.

I gritted my teeth and began combing out my wet mane.

"Are you up for talking?" He asked solemnly.

I sighed, "I think so."

"Do you remember the day you asked me about the other girls?"

I felt the buried emotions rise within me, my eyes welling with tears. "Yes," I replied tightly.

* * *

The mean girls had gone too far, particularly their ringleader, Tabitha. She was a redheaded vixen with catlike green eyes and the body of a Victoria's Secret model. It was hatred at first sight.

For months she kept hinting about a shared history with Adrien every time we were in the same room together, as well as his supposed Lothario reputation. I had witnessed none of this for myself, as I was at a disadvantage being the new kid in school. I barely had any friends aside from Adrien and his crew...my drama people and I were tight, but Adrien was really all I had.

He was never anything other than a perfect gentleman and I couldn't assume anything else other than Tabitha and her twat-posse were jealous that I, a mere nobody, had won the heart of the school's most desirable boy.

I couldn't take the snide remarks and veiled threats anymore, so I decided to ask the subject of the speculation himself.

His Bronco was being worked on again and we met by my car at the end of the day so I could give him a ride home.

"Hello, my beautiful songbird." Adrien scooped me into his arms kissing me soundly.

His scent was soothing and arousing all at once and enveloped in his arms I felt complete.

He framed my face with his hands, "What's wrong? You were smiling when I saw you at lunch, now you look stressed."

I bit him delicately on the chin before responding, "I'm okay, I just..." I sighed, "I need to talk to you about something and I don't want you to be mad, because I've been dealing with it for months and I probably should have talked to you immediately." I felt his fingertips tighten reflexively against my scalp.

"Has someone been messing with you, Luce?"

"Yes. But, come on and get in the car and we can talk on the way to your house." I propelled him towards the passenger side of my little, red Pontiac.

His jaw flexed with anger and I was even more nervous about this conversation.

Once I pulled out of the parking lot and made the turn in the direction of his house, I reluctantly continued, "I've been hearing things...about you. Pretty much ever since it became public knowledge we were together."

"From whom?" Was all he said.

"Those two, blonde bubble heads and that ginger tramp, Tabitha." I watched his fists clench in his lap at this revelation.

"And what have they said?" He ground out.

"That you only date girls until they give up their virginity, then you dump them. Tabitha alluded to you two having been involved. They say other awful things to me, but attacks on me I can deal with." I glanced over to see his knuckles still white and his jaw set.

I took a risk and reached over to touch his face and, to my relief, he relaxed and pushed into my hand, grabbing it and pressing his lips against my palm and wrist.

"Luce, I am so sorry you've been going through this alone. I wish you had said something sooner."

I pulled into his parents' long, winding driveway and cut the engine. Adrien got out first and came around to get my door, interlacing our fingers as we entered the miniature mansion.

"Are your parents home?" I whispered, not knowing why.

He answered against my temple, holding me close, "No, are they ever?"

"I'll make you a snack, if you want."

He grinned, massaging his fingers into my hair, "You're gonna make me a sammich, woman?"

I giggled and ducked under his arm, hurrying into the kitchen where he cornered me, lifting me up onto the counter to stand between my thighs.

Palm to palm, he leaned his forehead against mine, "Listen, Luce...you need to know that I did date Tabitha. She was my girlfriend all sophomore and junior year...and she is the spawn of Satan. She's not accustomed to things not going her way and until me, she'd never been dumped before."

"And the others?" It wasn't adding up in my mind that he had been in a relationship, yet supposedly deflowered all of those girls.

"In the past. I'm not that guy anymore. You're the only thing that matters to me. Everything is different with you, Luce." He cupped my face and nuzzled his lips into mine, effectively drugging me.

* * *

"I have interesting parents, wouldn't you say?"

I was perplexed by the topic change and I said so.

"I promise it's related, Luce."

I huffed out a breath, "Yeah, I mean...I think over the course of nine months I saw them maybe five or six times."

He nodded sadly, "Yeah, so here I was just a kid and I was left home alone in that big, empty house. A lot. They were always traveling for work. I met Tabitha and she was a force of nature. I was completely infatuated." He scooted back to lean against his pillows, looking up at the ceiling as he continued.

"I never had trouble getting girls, but I hadn't really done much at that point, you know? Tabitha took my virginity and that was enough to make me do whatever she wanted.

It started a few months after we had been dating when she took me to a party, got me drunk and told me she thought it would be hot to watch me with another girl. I was *sixteen*! I thought I'd hit the lottery by having a kinky girlfriend...but then it happened again. And again. And again...until every couple of weeks Tabitha had someone else she wanted me to seduce and she would coach me on how to do it. Sometimes she would have me draw it out a while to really get the girl attached before going in for the kill...it didn't take long for me to realize how sick and wrong it was and I was absolutely miserable.

Then one day, just an ordinary Saturday morning, I walked into my voice teacher's house a little earlier than I usually did. That day changed my life forever." He looked over at me and smiled, but it was bittersweet.

I motioned for him to continue, unable to speak past the lump in my throat.

"That day I went straight to Tabitha's and dumped her. She had taken the purity of what was supposed to be first love and poisoned it, making it—and me—ugly and twisted. When I saw you that first time, I understood what love is *really* supposed to feel like...light, free, and clean.

What I hadn't realized is that Tabitha had documented *everything*. She'd been there at every tryst she arranged, taking pictures, filming and writing everything in a journal that I never knew about. She tried scaring you off on her own, but she underestimated you. So, she came to me and threatened to go public with it all if I didn't break up with you and get back together with her and resume our games."

Fucking bitch! I seethed. "I need a little time to digest this, Aydo." There was a slight quiver in my voice.

"I understand," He said thickly.

He stood to leave, looking defeated, but I got up and blocked his path, "Hey, we're okay—I'm just overloaded with information and, frankly, I'd like to track Tabitha down and punch her in the cunt."

His laugh was weak, but his relief was palpable. "I'll just go grab a shower and give you a quick break, then...if that's okay?"

I squeezed his hands reassuringly, "Thank you, I just need to find my Zen. I'll be fine by the time you're finished."

His eyes glittered with unshed tears as he made his way to our bathroom and closed the door behind him.

I collapsed on my bed and glowered at the ceiling, enumerating all of the ways in which I would torture and maim Tabitha if I ever saw her again. Sick, distorted bitch.

I closed my eyes, concentrating on my breathing, as I emptied my mind of all the negative thoughts that had set up residence. I knew I had to let it go for my own sake...and for Adrien's, too.

Grabbing my phone, I checked Facebook and Twitter. We had several new follows and comments after tonight's show, as well as photos people had taken during the performances.

I smiled to myself as I saw several photos people had taken during the impromptu duet between Adrien and me, and the feedback was mostly positive.

> **"OMG, so cute! So happy for you two! <3<3<3"**

> **"I'm SO jelis!"**

More of the same over and over, yet one comment stood out:

> **"Looking good Adrien, very hot. The years have not been so kind to Lustella. She needs to disappear."**

The fuck? This was from a Twitter user and the name and photo didn't reveal much upon further inspection.

I sighed and made sure my phone alarm was set and plugged in on my bedside table.

When Adrien came out of the bathroom in just fitted boxer briefs and my t-shirt, I had very little control over my eyes as they admired his long, muscular legs and skimmed over the growing bulge just behind the cotton.

He made a soft growling sound at my leer and hurriedly slid under the covers, rolling onto his side towards me.

The gap between our beds felt like an ocean of distance, but I stayed firmly planted under my own sheets and comforter.

"I'm glad I know the truth, Aydo. The way it all played out just never sat well with me, but I was so wrecked afterwards, I didn't want to believe what my gut was telling me." I reached over and switched off the lamp. There was a soft bluish light dusting over us from the small TV in our room, which Adrien had turned on and left at a low volume. It was some kind of nature program about ocean creatures. I didn't care what it was, really, but he remembered I couldn't fall asleep without the TV on.

"I would've done just about anything to protect you, Luce. Still would. With your parents' situation being what it was, you being the new girl your senior year...I was afraid of what a direct attack from Tabitha would've done to you. I thought it would have affected you worse than what I did. We never came right out and said we loved each other...you always held such a tight rein on your emotions that I guess I didn't really think you cared as much as you did. When I saw you at school that following day, I knew immediately how badly I had screwed up. Watching you in agony like that gutted me...I should have fought back harder for you. For *us*." He had flipped back his covers and sat on the edge of his mattress nearest me.

I was breathing rapidly, tears stinging the back of my throat as I rose up and crawled out of my bed and onto his lap, straddling his hips. Anchoring my fingers in his hair, I tilted his face up to me, tiny streams of saltwater spilling from my eyes as I sealed my lips over his.

"Hush," I whispered.

He gripped my waist, almost bruising, drawing deeply from my mouth and sliding his tongue against mine.

He kissed the tears from my cheeks, along my jaw, the sensitive skin below my ear, and rubbed his scruffy chin against the delicate flesh where my neck and shoulder met. My nerves sparkled, sending a beam of arousal straight to my center, and I jerked in his arms, effectively rubbing against his erection in the process.

His moan vibrated on my skin and he raised his head again to claim my lips, sliding one hand up, cupping the back of my head to hold me captive as he plundered my mouth. As one, we maneuvered further back on the bed and Adrien flipped me over, pulling one of my legs up to wrap around him. I dropped my other knee to the side, nestling him between my thighs and aligning my core with his hot, hard ridge. I was overheating with desire, but I didn't care as I pulled up the back of his—*my*—shirt to feel his smooth, feverish skin. He released my lips just long enough to yank it off over his head and toss it to the floor. The flinty look in his eyes was all the encouragement I needed to remove my—*his*—shirt as well.

His jaw went slack as he took me in: all alabaster skin adorned with ink. I was dimly aware that he'd never actually come close to seeing me naked, never mind the fact he'd *never* touched my breasts.

"Perfect." Was all he said before lowering his head, sucking one aching nipple into his mouth and grazing his callused palm over the other. The dual sensation made me arch, setting my nails into his shoulders.

He placed steaming, open-mouthed kisses on my skin as he made his way back to my lips, sucking my tongue into his mouth and grinding his length against my throbbing clit.

I sighed into his kiss, muttering, "Again."

He obliged, rolling his hips as I angled my pelvis to match his rhythm. *Yesssss....*

It was just the amount of pressure I needed as we rocked against each other, our tongues locked in a heated battle, his hands roaming freely over my body as he'd never done before, fingers clutching into the firmness of my ass.

My lower abs clenched as my orgasm erupted like tiny thunder and I swallowed Adrien's moan as he followed me over the edge, the streams of his semen leaking through his underwear to make a mess on us both.

We gasped for air together, kissing and holding each other as we were overcome with laughter.

"We just dry-humped." I snickered, bussing his cheek.

His answering chuckle warmed my heart, "Well, not entirely dry...sorry about that."

I shrugged as much as I was able being all tangled with Adrien, "Dry-humping is serious business...sometimes things don't stay dry." I couldn't help my giggles.

He carefully extricated himself from me, looking down at the large wet patch on the front of his boxer-briefs and the matching one on the front of my pajama bottoms.

I laughed so hard, tears came to my eyes and he joined in. We seriously could have been in high school with this kind of activity.

It was awesome.

I joined him in the bathroom to clean ourselves up, Adrien giving me a pair of boxer shorts to wear with his shirt. I wasn't sure how I would explain what had happened to my PJs. He donned a fresh pair of boxer briefs, *my* shirt, and this time, we curled up in his bed together.

I rested my head on the dip between his chest and shoulder, one leg across his hips, my hand on his belly...I was intrigued by the ridges and valleys of the muscles I found there and he had to halt my exploration more than once.

"That was..." He trailed off.

"Yeah, it really was." I answered and leaned up to press a kiss against the pulse under his chiseled jawbone.

He rested his lips in my hair, inhaling me. "Luce?"

"Mmm?" My eyelids were starting to droop.

"I meant what I said earlier tonight. I love you. Always did."

I squeezed him tight, "I love you, too."

His hold intensified around me as he released the breath he'd been holding as he waited for my reply.

We had a lot to figure out tomorrow.

9

I awoke to the soft strumming of a guitar and Adrien's husky morning baritone singing along, sometimes full phrases, sometimes just humming.

I rolled towards the sound, blinking and shoving my hair—which I had forgotten to braid last night—off of my face.

"I couldn't believe my eyes when I saw you standing there..." He hummed through a few mores lines, *"Songbird...flew back into my arms..."*

"Hmmm, whatever could that be about?" I yawned.

Adrien jerked and looked over his shoulder, "Hey, good morning. Did I wake you?" He stood and stretched, still wearing my shirt and his underpants, before setting his guitar in its case and crawling across the bed to lie on top of me.

"Not really. It was a nice way to wake up...I must look awful right now." I tried to smooth down my errant waves that were spread in a tangle all over the pillow.

He leaned down and kissed me lazily, "You look perfect."

As Adrien started to move away, I snaked my arms around his neck and yanked him back to my mouth, nipping and biting at his lips until he gave me his tongue.

He groaned, pulling the covers off of me to let his hands roam over my skin, slipping under my—*his*—boxers to grip the globes of my ass and grind his morning wood against my sensitive core.

I bucked against him, sucking on his tongue and seeking his bare skin with my wandering fingers. His heartbeat thundered against my chest, mirroring mine exactly, as we feverishly groped and sucked and kissed each other into madness.

"Luce—" I cut him off by biting his earlobe.

"What? Ohhhhh…" His hot breath in my ear had me wet and squirming.

"Clothes…off…now…I need to taste you." Before I could react, Adrien was lifting the hem of my—*his*—shirt, baring my aching breasts to the morning light and his hungry gaze. The boxers went next and I was completely exposed, but not remotely self-conscious.

Adrien stared at me for a full minute, biting his lower lip in appreciation, "Damn, Luce." He returned to me, taking a long draw from my lips before blazing a trail down my throat to my breasts where he laved and teased my nipples into hard peaks, then delved his tongue into my navel before setting his teeth into the taught skin over my hipbones.

I cried out, my arousal heightening with the slight pain from his bite, then gasped in surprise when his breath touched me briefly before he swept his tongue across my clit. I grabbed fistfuls of his hair as he loved me with his mouth, slipping one long finger inside to caress the sensitive ridges in the front of my channel.

"More," I muttered and he increased the pressure of his caress, adding one more finger as he continued to suck and flick my sensitive bud with the tip of his tongue.

My back arched off the mattress as I came apart in a gushing, shuddering mess.

Adrien kissed his way back up to me, nuzzling against my neck and once again covering my body with his. My pulse thudded in my ears as my muscles still quivered and shook.

"Now *that*—" I cupped his jaw and kissed his eyelids, nose and lips, "—is an even *better* way to wake up."

He laughed huskily into my mouth, "You're incredible to watch when you come."

"Kinda makes you wish you had tried to get me into bed before, huh?" I teased.

He leaned back, resting his weight on his forearms, "No—I stand by what I said. As much as I loved you and wanted you back then, I still don't think I would have fully appreciated such a gift."

I smiled up at him, "Speaking of gifts...shall I return the favor?" I waggled my eyebrows suggestively.

He groaned and I felt his member twitch against my lower belly, "As much as I am loving that idea...No. This was all about you this morning. I have a lot of making up to do."

"Are you sure?" I reached down to cup him through his shorts.

He growled and batted my hand away, "I'm taking a cold shower now, before I do something selfish." He kissed me once, sucking hard on my lower lip before jumping out of bed and hurrying to the bathroom where I heard the water turn on shortly after.

I purred in satisfaction for a few minutes before sitting up to find my comb and work the knots out of my hair.

* * *

Adrien and I managed to get dressed with minimal groping and he sported my shirt again with fitted, distressed jeans and his favorite Chuck Taylors.

I caved and left his shirt on as well—added a bra, thank you very much—paired it with a flowy, white gauze skirt, and hemp wedge sandals. I surveyed the loose shirt in the mirror for a moment before adding a wide belt around my waist.

"You certainly don't dress the same," Adrien met my look in the mirror, his chin resting on my shoulder.

"Oh, yeah? Got something to say about it?" I smirked, reaching behind me to tickle his belly.

He backed away, hands in front of him, "No way, not me. This look is just...very *you*. Back in the day, you dressed kind of uptight."

I gasped and frowned, ready to be offended, but then I paused to give it serious thought. *He has a point*, I mused. In high school I wanted to blend in, so I stuck with polo-neck, fitted shirts and V-neck sweaters with...I gagged slightly...*khakis.*

I shuddered in horror, spinning to face him, "You, sir, are absolutely correct. Let's just say that I took Jim Morrison's advice and found my 'will to be weird'." I twined my arms around his neck.

His hands automatically went to my hips, bending his head to kiss my nose, "This suits you better...particularly that mysterious flush to your complexion." His grinned was roguish air.

"Cheeky!" I shoved him away, returning to the task of packing up my things.

"Um...Luce?"

The note of worry in Adrien's voice gave me pause, "What's wrong?"

He looked uncertain before he asked, "What are you going to tell Oscar?"

My mind was utterly blank and it must have been all over my face, so he prompted, "Your boyfriend...Oscar? You mentioned him back in Tulsa."

I blushed in furious embarrassment, "Yeah...there's no Oscar, Aydo."

His hands flew to his face, eyes wide in shock, "Well, I declare, Miss Lustella, did you tell a falsehood?"

"Shut up," I grumbled, slapping my belongings into my suitcase a little less delicately than I should.

He snickered behind me, but said no more.

Being a guy, he had all of his belongings—besides their instruments and equipment—stuffed into a backpack. It was a decently-sized camping backpack, but a single bag nonetheless.

For me a makeup case, a suitcase, a large canvas tote, and my cross-body purse *were* considered packing lightly.

I had received a text earlier from Nova saying they were all going to meet up for brunch at Clover Grill a few blocks from our hotel. I was told to bring the *Loft* boys along. I jostled Kyle, Toko and Andy (I think his name is Andy...he doesn't really speak) so they could get dressed and come with us.

"I'll help you put your stuff in the van, Luce." Adrien snicked my makeup box and canvas tote from my hands, telling the boys we would be back in a few to retrieve them.

"Thank you." I pecked him on the cheek as he slung my tote over his shoulder and interlaced his fingers with mine as we strolled to the elevator.

He merely winked in response, but it was such a sexy wink that I cornered him in the elevator and kissed him silly.

I stepped out into the lobby, cool as you please, with a disheveled Adrien hurrying behind me.

"And you say *I'm* cheeky?!" He rumbled behind me.

I giggled and kept walking straight to the van. Freed from our burdens, we held hands again and skipped— yes, skipped—back inside to round up the bandmates.

* * *

"This would look better on me," I announced as I snatched the straw fedora Adrien had put on in our hotel room off of his head to place it on mine.

"Not going to argue with you," He grinned and smacked a kiss on my cheek, holding his phone out in front of us to snap a photo.

I smiled at his profile as he uploaded the picture to his page and tagged me in it.

I looked at Nova across the table to see her beaming at me. I gave her a one-shouldered shrug and ducked my head, my cheeks heating.

Our combined groups nearly took up the entire diner and really livened up the place with our eclectic garb, various piercings and tattoos.

Rhys, Nova, Adrien and I all shared a booth. It warmed my heart to see Nova and Rhys all loved up. They don't like being apart, but Rhys's job doesn't leave much room for him to be able to travel with us. Fortunately, this tour is only for a few months and Nova has an awesome friend like me to make arrangements for her hubby to come and see her while we're gone!

"We need to compare schedules," Adrien's lips by my ear shook me out of my musings.

I took a long sip of my coffee and nodded, digging my phone out of my purse to bring up my calendar. "Yes, let's do that now."

As it turned out, we had several locations in common—a fact which I noticed Adrien and I both released a held breath upon discovery.

My caravan was headed to Utah, while *Loft* would be in New Mexico, and then we would be together in Colorado after that.

My tour began June first and we already had a month behind us, having started in the Midwest, kicking off in Ohio. We would finish at home in Portland on September first. *Loft's* tour went to October first and they would be finishing off at home as well in San Diego.

Fate certainly had conspired to bring us together again—a fact I became more and more certain of as I compared calendars with Adrien.

I wondered, with no little amount of concern, what I was going to tell my dad.

10

Later that evening, we all stood in the middle of the New Orleans airport after having just cleared security. Our gates, however, were in opposite wings.

"I'm just afraid if I let you go now that I'm going to wake up and realize none of this ever happened." Adrien tucked some strands of hair that had escaped my braid behind my ears.

I shook my head and kissed him reassuringly for what felt like the hundredth time, "I will see you in ten days in Denver, then we'll be together there, Aspen *and* Boulder, Aydo."

He nodded and held me against him, squeezing me until I heard my spine crackle and pop.

"I love you." His kiss was long and deep, intended to hold me over for our time apart.

"I love *you*." I tugged on his bottom lip and gave him a playful shove and a lingering pat on the bum which made him laugh.

I quickly hugged Kyle, Toko and Andy (his name *is* Andy for sure), then made myself turn away and join my colorful family of artists as we made our exeunt towards our gate. Rhys's gate was in the same direction so Nova and he could have a few more precious minutes together.

* * *

"You had sex!" Nova accused as soon as we settled into our seats.

"No, *you* had sex...I merely engaged in heavy petting." I replied serenely.

When she didn't respond, I glanced over to see Nova staring me down with a raised eyebrow.

"Okay, so he went down on me this morning, but that is *all*!" I hurried.

Nova raised her chin and studied my face for a long moment before she was seemingly satisfied that I had been completely forthcoming.

After we were in the air, she asked, "How do you feel about all of this?"

I filled her in on everything Adrien had revealed to me the night before about Tabitha, the blackmail and the other girls.

When I finished, she was aghast, "That's some fucked up *Dangerous Liaisons* shit, right there."

I nodded, "No kidding. I knew back then what a wench Tabitha was, but I had no idea how deeply it ran. Girl had issues...and she rubbed it in my face after he broke up with me."

* * *

I had spent the whole weekend crying, but knew I couldn't stay home from school, so I forced myself to get up and go on Monday morning. I tied my hair back in a ponytail, didn't bother with makeup, nor did I try with my clothes which were a black hoodie, jeans and my purple Converse sneakers.

Let him see me like this, *I thought bitterly as I swallowed back a wave of misery.*

My one and only other close friend, Isobel, stuck by my side all day—thankfully we had all of the same classes together, except the last one—so she shielded me from Adrien as much as possible.

In each class he was in, I could feel him watching me, but I wouldn't look at him. I kept my head down and pretended to be invisible.

By the time the end of the day rolled around and I entered my last class, I actually felt pretty stable but halted just outside the doorway.

Tabitha was making an obscene display of making out with Adrien on the other side of the threshold, running her hands all over him and messing up his hair.

I froze and didn't know what to do. I couldn't look away, though I desperately wanted to gouge out my own eyes with a blunt object.

Thankfully one of my classmates, Benny, looked up, saw what was happening, and swooped in to rescue me. He was a gentle soul and had been a good friend to me throughout the school year. He marched past Tabitha and Adrien, pulled me into his side and walked me to my desk, acting as a human barrier for me, blocking the horror show happening a few feet away.

He kept my back towards them and ducked to get my attention, "Luce, look at me. Don't look at them. Look at me, okay?"

My chest started heaving as I began to hyperventilate, the tears leaking out and dripping onto my sweatshirt.

"No, no, no...come here." Benny tucked my head into his chest and swayed in place, rubbing circles on my back.

"Is she okay?" I dimly heard Adrien's voice ask.

"What the fuck do you think, O'Rourke? Just stay away from her—you've done enough. I knew you

would screw this up sooner or later. You should have just left her alone." I had never heard Benny speak with such anger or vehemence.

My breathing calmed and I was able to disengage myself from Benny, "Thank you, B. Thank you so much." I slid into my seat and, fortunately, Benny's was right behind me so I felt well-guarded. Adrien was on the opposite end of the row from us and his eyes burned holes into the side of my face.

Once the final bell rang, Benny was up and out of his seat, grabbing my arm and my backpack to escort me to my car.

"Thanks again, B. I'm okay now."

"You're welcome. Let me know if he bothers you, okay? Or if you need anything else, Luce..." Benny closed my car door and waited until I pulled out of the parking lot. I glanced in the rear view mirror and noticed Adrien watching from the open classroom window.

* * *

The flight from New Orleans to Salt Lake City was short and soon we were, once again, loading up in a rented van and heading to our hotel.

It was after midnight, so we didn't say much as we settled in and got ready for bed.

My phone dinged from the bedside table—I changed it from the fart noise, much to Nova's disappointment—and I dropped everything to grab it.

Aydo: Are you there yet? Are you there yet?

Me: Yes…video call?

My phone immediately lit up and I was laughing as I answered, "I'm not naked yet, simmer down!"

Aydo brought his phone all the way to his eye and then pulled it back so I could see his whole face, "Damn it."

"I'm just getting ready for bed, what are you doing?" I propped my phone up on the bathroom counter and began my nightly grooming ritual.

"I'm in bed, working on a new song. It's going to be difficult to sleep without you next to me."

"Oh, please! After one night?" His quiet declaration made my stomach flutter despite my outward scoff.

"That was the most peaceful sleep I can ever recall having, Luce. I used to love to keep you out long enough so we'd end up falling asleep together." He'd shifted so it looked like he was on his side looking at me lying next to him.

I patted my face dry, "I remember. You weaseled sleepovers out of my dad on many occasions, which is quite the accomplishment with his background."

"I'll say. Former military *and* Secret Service? I'm lucky I lived past our first date. How is he doing?" Adrien yawned.

"He's wonderful. He met a lovely woman named Alice and they got married last year. They are actually staying at my house while I'm away to look after my kids." I dabbed retinol cream under my eyes.

"Kids?" Adrien's eyes were large on my phone screen.

I giggled, "My dog and cat, you dork! Edgar and Mata. Spend some more time stalking my Facebook and you'll see an abundance of photos featuring them."

"Thank the gods! I am not ready to be a step-father."

I arched a brow, "Getting ahead of ourselves, aren't we?"

He stared intently at me through the lens, "Make no mistake; you're going to marry me, Lustella MacLean."

I laughed nervously and rapidly changed the subject, "So, you'll have to meet the fur balls when we're all in Portland together, yeah?"

He studied me, ultimately deciding to let my evasion slide, "Yes, definitely."

We continued chatting as I finished with myself and settled into bed, wearing his shirt and boxers once again.

I held the phone in my hand as I rested on my side, "Wait until I fall asleep?"

"Of course. I love you, Luce." His voice drifted soothingly from the speaker.

"I love you, Aydo. Goodnight."

"Goodnight, my little songbird."

* * *

Salt Lake City was surprisingly receptive. I'd had my reservations, considering...you know, religious persons known to inhabit the area.

The show went well the night before and Nova and I were looking forward to some sightseeing and hiking. The beauty of this tour was that it was also doubling as a vacation. We scheduled everything so we would have time to explore new places and have adventures while we were in strange lands.

We spent the morning and afternoon in Arches National Park and it was absolutely stunning. I was generally a happy and open person, but since reconnecting with Adrien, I was looking at the world around me through new eyes. I actually wept at the sight of the precarious, towering formations in the arid, coppery landscape.

"I'm so not ready to leave here, Vava."

"Gotta go to Provo, Stel. Aren't you eager to move along with this part of our trip so we can get to Denver?" Nova elbowed me in the side as we made our way back to the van.

I smiled thoughtfully, "Yeah, I guess I am. I keep waiting for the other shoe to drop, though, you know?"

She sighed, rubbing the shaved side of her head, "I know. I don't blame you, but please don't self-sabotage, okay? Just see how this all plays out."

I nodded, kicking rocks out of my way as we went.

* * *

Another city, another airport, another van. At last, we were in Denver. I looked up at the white-peaked roof of the airport, thinking it looked smaller than it did when I was a kid and came here to visit my uncle Rob, the pot-smoking Dead-head. May he rest in peace.

My phone dinged.

> **Aydo: Just checked in at the hotel. Had to switch reservations so we could be in the same one as you.**
>
> **Me: Oh, good! We're just loading up the van, we'll be there soon.**
>
> **Aydo: Can. Not. Wait.**

My cheeks warmed as we hopped in and left the airport.

As we entered our hotel, I saw Adrien before he saw me. He sat on a sofa in the lobby, his ankle resting on his opposite knee and twitching furiously.

I stopped and waited, but not for very long. The moment his scanning eyes arrested on me, I felt it all over. Thundering butterflies erupted in my stomach and my knees wobbled as we crossed to each other.

Adrien grabbed my upper arms, holding me away from him to inspect me from head to toe, "You're here. You're okay?"

I laughed, "You have talked to me every day we've been apart, you goof. Yes, I am fine. Now, greet me properly!"

Pulling me close, Adrien cupped the back of my neck with one hand and placed the other on the small of my back. Surprising a shriek out of me, he dipped me low, pressing a warm, lingering kiss on my lips before setting me back on my feet.

"How was that?" His lush, green eyes twinkled with amusement.

"That was satisfactory, thank you." I harrumphed.

He proffered his arm, snagging my tote and makeup box with his other hand, "May I escort you to your room, Mademoiselle?"

"You may." I slid my hand through the crook in his elbow.

* * *

"I was wondering," Adrien began as he helped Nova and me into our room, "how sleeping arrangements are going to work?"

I whipped my head around at him, "And just what do you mean, sir?"

Nova chuckled and pretended to be engrossed in arranging her things.

He stepped closer to me, brushing my cheek with his knuckles, "We don't have the same level of privacy this time around, and I was just wondering..." He trailed off.

I shook my head at him, "Aydo, I am going to have to cock block you. I'm not leaving Nova alone in our room, you can't stay with us—that would be weird—and I'm not sleeping in a room full of dudes. You're just going to have to be satisfied with stolen kisses and lingering looks until we *can* be alone." I brushed my lips over his chin.

He sighed, resting his forehead against mine, "You're right, I apologize. I'm being selfish again, aren't I?"

"Not entirely. I would love nothing more than to be cuddled up with you at night, but it's just not going to work this time. Let me get settled in here and then we can all go grab some food, okay?" I combed his silky hair off of his face with my fingers, massaging his temples. His eyes closed in bliss, but he nodded.

"See you in a bit," He kissed me between my eyebrows and left the room.

"He's got it so bad," Nova spoke up from her unobtrusive corner.

I flopped back on my bed, "He's not the only one."

11

Toko glanced around before getting my attention, "Luce, can I talk to you for a sec?"

"What's up?" I smiled and sat down next to him in the restaurant we'd chosen, waiting for the others to catch up.

"I had an idea for something to do at the show tomorrow night and wondered if you're game?" He spoke quietly as if he didn't want to be overheard.

"Tell me."

"How would you feel about doing a drum solo during our set?"

I cocked my head, "You have a doumbek?"

"No, but I was thinking it would be cool to play the Middle Eastern rhythms on my drums. Kind of tie everything together?"

"I am definitely game!" We high-fived and shook on it.

"Game for what?" Adrien interrupted.

Toko and I looked up at him in surprise. I gathered he wanted to keep it a secret so I jumped up and slipped my arms around Adrien, "Oh, nothing. Just talking about music."

He narrowed his eyes in suspicion, "Okay."

* * *

"Ladies and gentlemen, our drummer, Toko, has been cooking up some new rhythms and wanted to give them a try this evening...put your hands together!" Adrien stepped to the side, letting the lights focus on Toko's platform.

I hid backstage, waiting for my signal. We'd had a devil of a time trying to put this together last minute, especially with Adrien seldom letting me out of his sight and I hoped it went well. Drum solos were something Nova and I did often, but never like this...it was certainly going to be interesting.

Toko started thrashing and pounding out some wild and showy rhythms, I had about a minute until he gave me my four, hard thumps on the base to let me know I needed to shimmy my ass out into the spotlight.

I had changed my costume up a little bit, switching out my voluminous harem pants for a glittery, turquoise mermaid-style skirt and removed my headdress so my hair flowed freely around me.

Boom, boom, boom, boom!

Out I went, applause soon following when the audience picked up on our game. Toko vibrated his cymbals and I stood, grinning over my shoulder at Adrien, starting a tiny earthquake with my glutes and hips.

I mused to myself that this skirt was an excellent choice as the sequins caught the light and gave the illusion of serpentine skin flowing over my lower half.

Toko transitioned into chiftitelli and I followed right along with him, moving around the stage and spinning my way towards Adrien, whose eyes dragged over my undulating form with raw hunger.

"So *that's* what you two were whispering about all day."

I winked, "Good surprise?"

He nodded, biting his lower lip.

My lower belly clenched and I felt the air shift between us.

"Later." I promised and pivoted away as Toko switched smoothly to baladi.

* * *

After *Loft* finished their set and moved their instruments and equipment offstage, Adrien stalked me.

I backed away from him, moving deeper and deeper backstage, hiding behind the thick, black curtains. The sounds from the front were muffled, but we were—more or less—completely alone.

"I think you were jealous of my secret meetings with Toko," I spoke from behind a wall of sturdy velveteen.

I shrieked a little, startled by Adrien whipping the curtain aside in his predatory pursuit as he kept moving forward into my personal space, forcing me to walk backwards until my shoulders bumped the wall.

"I won't deny it." He replied in a low tone, flattening his right palm against my breastbone, his left arm braced by my head.

Heat radiated from his hand and danced over my skin, and I reached up to thread my fingers in his hair.

Keeping the pressure firm, he slid his hand down between my breasts, over my taut abdomen to my thigh, coaxing my skirt up high enough to slip underneath and brush his fingertips over my pulsing clit through my lacy boy shorts.

I gasped, arching into him and pulling his face down for a long, drugging kiss as I removed one of my hands from his hair and reached down to cup him through his jeans.

He jerked his hips and bit down on my lip as he growled in his throat, "I don't think I can stop myself from being selfish right now, Luce."

I ran my tongue over his jaw, nipping his neck and earlobe, "Me either."

I used both hands to free him, digging a condom out of his pocket and slipping it over his steely, hot erection before returning to his mouth to slide my tongue against his.

Adrien's breathing stuttered in his chest as he grabbed hold of the lacy barrier between us and ripped it from my body, sliding both hands underneath my skirt to grip my ass and lift me so I could wrap my legs around his waist as he pressed me firmly against the concrete wall.

"You're so wet and ready for me, Luce." Adrien's mouth was buried against my throat as he eased inside of me.

We just held each other for a moment, allowing me to adjust to his size, my muscles clenching around him like a fist.

I framed his face with my hands, "I'm ready for you to move, Aydo."

He rocked once and we both closed our eyes at the delicious friction. He did it again and I thudded my head against the wall.

"Aydo!" I tugged his hair.

He smiled through hazy eyes, licking into my mouth until I trapped it with my teeth and sucked, making him moan and pump his hips more urgently.

I matched his rhythm as best I could in such a perilous position, rolling my pelvis and grinding against him to quicken my own release.

"Oh, god...Luce, you're so tight and if you keep doing *that*, I won't last."

My orgasm ripped through me, shattering me into a thousand tiny pieces as he swallowed my groan with his kiss.

As I trembled with aftershocks, Adrien buried his face in my hair and stiffened against me, a low keening leaving his throat as he pulsed and erupted in ecstasy.

We were coated in a light sheen of sweat, our breathing loud and unstable as we pressed light kisses to each other's faces and mouths, whispering soft and tender words.

Adrien lowered me to the ground, slipping out of me and disposing of the condom as I settled my skirt back around my legs.

When his pants were securely fastened he returned, taking me in his arms.

I tilted my face for his kiss, our lips slanting over one another's, slow and savoring, before we gingerly made our way back to the dressing rooms to retrieve my cover up and join our group out in the audience.

Before we reached our table, Adrien stopped moving.

I turned in concern, "What's wrong?"

He just stared at me, that old and achingly familiar look of breathless wonder all over his face, "Nothing at all. I just love you so much." He hugged me close, scenting my hair.

I laughed, my heart light and happy, my body sated and limber, "I love *you*."

* * *

"I didn't figure you for a cuddler." I smiled as Adrien nuzzled his lips into my hair—something he'd been doing all evening.

His answering grin was lazy and satisfied as he winked at me, "I can smell myself all over you."

I shook my head and looked away, blushing as my body heated with the memory of what we'd done just mere hours before. My pulse quickened as Adrien lightly traced patterns on my neck and I nipped at his fingers.

"Feisty, are we?" He rasped in my ear, causing my thighs muscles to clench.

"Down, boy." I pecked him on the nose.

"Okay, you two." Nova threw a dinner roll at me and I caught it.

"Ooh, cat-like reflexes!" I punctuated this taunt with a large bite from the piece of bread.

She rolled her eyes and smirked at me, shaking her head. "It's very late, and we should probably all get to bed if we want to spend quality time at Red Rocks tomorrow."

I bounced in my chair and squealed, making everyone at our table laugh.

* * *

I was in a familiar scenario again as Adrien trapped me against the wall just outside of my hotel room.

"Way too public, darling," I teased.

He captured my mouth, teasing the seam of my lips with his tongue until I opened to his invasion and pressed back against him, making him groan.

"Hey," He paused, cupping my face and looking into my eyes with a serious expression.

"What's up?" I rubbed circles on his back.

"Tonight was incredible, but I can't help but feel a little guilty. I feel like our first time together should have been…" He looked up searching for the words.

"Candles, massage oils, and Barry White?" I supplied jokingly.

"Well, more romantic for sure…maybe Puccini instead of Barry White." He revealed one dimple as he beamed at me.

I lifted my hands to toy with the soft curls at the nape of his neck, "Everything is just as it should be. There will be time later for longer, slower lovemaking. The truth is I *needed* that to happen…I couldn't wait."

"I missed you so much, Luce." He squeezed me against his chest, swaying back and forth.

Calmness settled over me along with a feeling of *rightness* and sanctuary as I melted into Adrien's body, inhaling his familiar scent which now carried hints of me. There in his arms, I was home at last.

12

"Are you sure this is okay?" I asked Nova, surveying the large hotel suite we were about to share with Adrien, Kyle, Toko, and Andy in Boulder.

"Of course it's okay. I get my own room and bathroom...and you get to have sinful romps out of wedlock with your long, lost love." With that, she carted her belongings into the nearest bedroom and staked her claim.

I leaned against the doorframe, smiling at her as she flailed around on the bed to mark her territory. "Vava, you're my most important person, so I want you to tell me if I'm not doing right by you, okay?"

"Just keep the noise down tonight, m'kay?" She teased.

"Perbert!" I spun on my heel and went to grab my stuff.

As I settled into the room I would share with Adrien for most of the week, I let my mind wander over the last several days. After our hurried coupling backstage in Denver, we hadn't had another opportunity to be intimate...not that he hadn't tried, the mischievous rake.

We'd spent a whole day at Red Rocks hiking and exploring; I'd even gotten Nova and Adrien to go rappelling with me.

I'd given a repeat performance with Toko at our other shows in Denver and Aspen—each time Toko took chances and tested me by slipping different rhythms into his set, but it was fun and challenging for my brain.

The boys sat me down and informed me that for the duration of our tours, provided we were in the same city, I would be singing with the band. I had laughed outright at their serious faces, but capitulated as soon as I was leveled with four sets of puppy-dog eyes. Crafty shits, they are.

There had been several more catty comments as more photos of us surfaced on the internet, most of them saying how fuckable Adrien was and how I— apparently—was not hot enough for him. I understood that women acted that way sometimes and I shouldn't take it personally, but being someone that had battled low self-esteem my whole life, it chafed a bit.

I didn't know if Adrien had seen any of it and I didn't want to ruin our perfect, little bubble of happiness. Unfortunately, I knew it was becoming necessary because they had escalated to a somewhat threatening degree.

All the time spent together talking and playing and laughing had solidified Adrien's and my rekindled love. Every time I looked over and caught him watching me with light in his eyes, I felt more at ease...all snide remarks from jealous females faded away from my mind. I also no longer panicked as much when Adrien made marriage proclamations to me privately or in front of our friends...or our audiences.

As if conjured from my thoughts, I was surrounded by his arms as he planted a heated kiss at the nape of my neck.

"Hey there, big boy." I turned and pressed my lips against his cheek.

"Hi," he whispered.

"I know it wasn't a long drive, but I feel like I've been in that van forever. Join me in the shower and conserve water?" I slipped out of his embrace and sauntered into the en suite bathroom.

I glanced over my shoulder in time to see a slow, seductive smile curve Adrien's beautiful lips as he came after me, already unbuttoning his shirt.

I flipped on the water to let it heat up and proceeded to strip out of my clothes, which was easy as flicking the straps of my sundress and letting it drop to the floor, leaving me bare.

Adrien's hazy green eyes roamed all over, warming my skin and causing a wave of desire to roll through me.

I backed into the shower and let the stream sluice down my chest and torso.

More quickly than I thought he could, Adrien shucked his clothes and joined me. He pressed his front to my back, the hardened ridge of his penis nestled against my lower back, his palms reaching around to cup and caress my breasts and nip gently at my ear lobe.

"This isn't candles and Puccini..." I gasped as Adrien slipped a finger between my folds to test my arousal.

"Don't care. Turn around." He urged.

He took my mouth, tasting and savoring my lips and tongue until I could barely breathe. Moving me out of the direct stream of water, Adrien made his way down, spending equal time at each breast, nipping at my ribcage, and finally settled on the floor of the shower and hitched my leg over his shoulder. That was all the warning I had before his tongue darted out to tease my clit making me gasp again and clutch at his hair.

I thudded my head against the tile, "Ayd-oh!"

His laughter vibrated against my sensitive flesh, adding to my pleasure as he licked into me.

As my tension built to the peak, he suddenly stopped.

"What the—?" I sounded a bit unhinged.

Adrien rose, kissing me deeply, "I need to be inside of you, Luce."

I nodded, reaching my hand down to stroke his shaft. He surged against my palm and I guided him towards me, but he halted again.

"Are you—?"

I caressed his cheek, "It's okay, Aydo. I'm on birth control."

I turned away from him and arched my lower back as Adrien moved forward and gently entered me from behind.

The angle was intense being the size he was, but the pleasure made my eyes roll back as he began to rock his hips.

Adrien reached down and grabbed my right leg, lifting it in the air. The intensity skyrocketed and I began to whimper as I felt my climax building quickly.

I glanced over my shoulder at Adrien's face and he was biting his lip, fighting for control. I reached between our legs and ran my nails lightly over his sensitive sac and his rhythm became wild and unfocused.

"Luce! Oh my god…" His heavy thrust pushed me over the edge of oblivion and I keened in my release, my cheek against the shower wall.

With just a few quick strokes, Adrien tumbled over after me, dropping my leg and wrapping his arms around my waist as he shuddered and spurted inside of me.

Panting and feverish, I turned in his arms and we held each other, swaying and kissing under the fall of water.

* * *

I liked being the big spoon, curling my body around Adrien's like a cat. We were snuggled up in bed talking when my phone rang.

Adrien glanced at the screen before handing it to me, "It's your dad."

Uh oh. "Hi daddy!"

"Hi, sweetheart. How's the tour?" I heard playful growling in the background and my heart ached.

"Is that Edgar in the background?"

"Yes, he's teasing Mata. But, how's the tour?"

"Good, we're on our last night in Boulder and heading to New Mexico tomorrow. Only Nevada and Washington left before I'm home again."

"I'll be glad to have you back safe and sound, honey. Everything is still fine here and the kids are great. Have you had any more run-ins with that boy?" My father's voice had taken a serious turn and I was reminded again why anyone I dated was terrified of him.

I chuckled, "Well, he's not a boy, Dad. And, actually...um, yes. I have." I grimaced, bracing for his outburst.

It never came.

"Dad, are you there?" I asked after a moment of stone silence.

"Yes, I'm here. I had this feeling in my gut when you mentioned seeing Adrien before that it was far from over." He sounded surprisingly calm.

"Well, there was much, much more to the story than I ever realized. Our tours have brought us together in several other spots, so we've been using the time to get everything out in the open and I'm giving him another chance. Are you okay with that?" I asked timidly.

Adrien carefully turned towards me without making a sound as I heard my dad take a deep breath and let it out.

"I trust your judgment and I know that Nova is probably keeping a close eye on you. That girl has good instincts and I know she'd speak up if something wasn't right."

I beamed, "You're right, she would."

"But," he started, "once you're home I want to know everything, okay?"

Adrien heard him say that and nodded at me, letting me know it was fine with him if I told.

"Yes, of course." I replied.

"Well, okay...I better let you get some rest and I'll check in with you a couple more times before you're home again. I love you, kiddo." Dad's voice was gruff.

"I love you most. Tell Alice hi and hug my babies for me."

We hung up.

"So..." Adrien began.

"Yeah. But, don't worry—I don't think he'll break anything valuable on your body." I teased, reaching my fingers out to tickle him.

He wrestled my hands away and kissed my laughing mouth.

"We've got this. I love you." I nuzzled his cheek.

Adrien rolled us over so he was now the big spoon, scenting my hair and holding me securely in his arms.

"I love you most."

I giggled and elbowed him.

* * *

Our time together in Boulder had been wonderful and I was very reluctant to part with it.

As I began gathering my things to pack, I decided to bring up the subject of the less-than-comforting posts on our pictures. We'd been doing so well with being open and honest, I felt I owed it to Adrien to let him know and tell him it *did* bother me.

"Hey, Aydo?" I asked distractedly as I scrolled down the page so I could show him the snarky comments that kept popping up, but I couldn't find any of them.

He came up behind me and dug his fingers into my tight neck and shoulders, "What's wrong?"

I moaned in bliss as he worked the knots out of my muscles, "Hmmm? Oh. Um…well, I was going to ask you if you had seen some of the comments on the recent photos posted of us online, but I don't see them now. There's stuff on my Facebook, too, though." I flipped to the *Candéo* page to the latest bits of vitriol.

He went still as his eyes scanned through the remarks. The last I'd glanced at had hinted at my needing to literally break a leg. *Nice.*

"I saw the stuff on my page and deleted them all. I won't allow any of that negative shit all over band's page, *especially* if they're directing it at you."

His tone put me on alert, "What aren't you telling me? Do you know who it was?" I shrugged him off and turn around. He looked pale.

He slanted his eyes away from me and I captured his chin between my thumb and forefinger, bringing my face close until he met my stare.

"Who is it, Aydo?"

He didn't answer me, but he didn't really need to. My intuition told me everything I needed to know and his silence confirmed it.

"You're still in contact with...*Tabitha*?" her name was poisonous on my tongue.

He grabbed my wrists, pleading with me, "*No*. But I have no control over who follows the public accounts for the band. I promise you, the only interaction I have with her is to delete anything she posts."

I clenched my jaw, remaining silent.

"I told you, Luce. She's fucked in the head—and she's tried pulling stuff online. I have blocked her many times, but she keeps opening new accounts under different names. And now that you and I are together again it probably set her off. In her eyes, *you* stole me from her. Of course she's going to try to mess with us." He tried to kiss me on the forehead, but I flinched away and my heart lurched at his wounded expression.

"No secrets, Aydo. That's what got us into such a mess before." I willed my heart rate to slow, uncurling my fisted hands against his chest.

He slumped, dropped his face to my shoulder. "I know; I'm so sorry. I am just so accustomed to getting rid of her posts that it didn't occur to me that I should tell you, or that you had even seen them. I didn't realize she'd already made her presence known on your pages. I wish—I want to protect you from that. I failed again."

I held him close, "You didn't fail at anything. Everything will be okay."

* * *

I stood in front of the floor-length mirror in the hallway of my house and smoothed my silver gown once more. It was prom night and I didn't have a date. I didn't want to go, but my Isobel refused to let me hide out and miss this "pivotal event" as she called it.

Isobel had been a transplant as well, only she'd arrived about a year before I did. Her date was her long-distance boyfriend Jensen who still lived in Missouri and attended the state college there on a football scholarship. He was a good guy and made me laugh when he said he would be honored to be the third wheel in our ménage a trois for prom.

I can do this, I told myself silently in the mirror. My dad came up behind me, beaming.

"You look stunning, kiddo."

I turned and looked up at him...my dad was the tallest man in the world, or, at least, that's how I always perceived him.

"Thanks, Daddy." I wrapped my arms around his waist as he kissed the top of my head. He released me to answer the door when the bell rang.

I returned to the mirror to check my hair and makeup and listened to the chatter of voices in the entryway; Isobel's voice was the loudest, as usual.

As I came around the corner, I stopped dead in my tracks. What the hell?

Isobel turned and grinned at me excitedly, "Surprise!" She gestured grandly to the tall and handsome stranger standing next to Jensen.

I walked forward, still confused. Jensen came to my rescue, "Luce, this is my best friend Christian. I thought you two would hit it off...no pressure, though. He's a good guy and can't resist a damsel in distress, especially beautiful ones in formal wear." He wrapped an arm around my shoulders and gave me an encouraging squeeze.

"Hi, Christian." I held out my hand, which he took and very chivalrously planted a kiss on my knuckles, surprising a giggle out of me.

"Luce, it's nice to meet you. I just want you to know, I was against keeping this a secret from you, but I

hope you'll do me the honor of letting me escort you this evening." His voice was pleasantly deep and he had open and friendly dark, brown eyes.

He wasn't quite as tall as my father or Adrien, but he had a broad chest and shoulders which indicated he was also a football player. He certainly filled out his tuxedo in a pleasing way and he was very easy on my eyes.

"Christian, I would love for you to be my escort. Your vest does match my gown perfectly, after all. Thank you for coming to my rescue." I took the arm he offered and we headed outside to take photos.

* * *

I thought back to that night and how Tabitha had spread various rumors around like I hired my date off of the internet, he was actually gay, or he was my cousin. I remembered Adrien watching me with Christian and the way Tabitha would run her hands all over him and kiss him, being sure that I saw everything. When I tried to sneak away down one of the hallways at school to avoid the line for the bathroom, I interrupted Tabitha giving Adrien a blow-job. After that, I ran back into the gym straight into Christian's arms.

I lost my virginity that night. Christian did his best to be noble and talk me out of it, but I was very persuasive and, in the end, it had been a wonderful first experience. And second...and third. I had been very motivated and Christian had been very accommodating.

I was jarred out of my reverie when Adrien shook me, "Luce? Luce? Where did you go on me?"

My emotions varied between horror and guilty pleasure as I thought first of Tabitha and her antics, quickly followed by Christian's attentions.

"I was just thinking about prom, actually." He blanched at my statement.

"Oh god, Luce."

"It's in the past, remember? Besides, my *whole* night wasn't ruined..." I said mysteriously, pulling away and moving towards the bed to organize my suitcase.

"Well, I'm glad. Just so you know...what you walked in on wasn't actually what it looked like. I was fighting her off of me, but she was digging those fake nails into me and not letting go." He sat down on the edge of the mattress to watch me at work.

I paused, reluctantly picturing that scene once more and let all of the details appear in my mind. His face had been twisted in pain, not pleasure and his hands had been pushing her away from him, not clutching her close.

I glanced over at him and nodded my assent, "I believe you."

"Who was that guy you came with anyway?" His voice held nothing but idle curiosity, but I didn't fully trust it.

"Oh, um...he was Isobel's boyfriend's friend from college." I *so* hoped the conversation didn't head where I feared it might. After seven years apart, clearly I had been with other people, but I didn't think it would be prudent for Adrien to know precisely *when* that had started.

I saw him nod out of the corner of my eye, sighing quietly in relief he didn't ask any more questions.

He surprised me again, however, when he said quietly, "it's not a pleasant thing for me to think about, but I realize I have no business being upset about men you chose to spend time with intimately."

It was my turn to simply nod and we said no more.

13

Our parting in Colorado had been more emotional than the others, but I knew that it was because of how much closer we had become over the weeks we'd spent together.

I worried about what the future would hold for us when our tours were over and we each had to return to our respective homes, but for now I had to focus on the present.

Presently, Nova was reading to me on her tablet while we cruised through the air to New Mexico, but if I was being honest with myself, my mind kept wandering to the various things that happened over the last several weeks.

* * *

Naked and tangled up in our sheets, Adrien and I lay side by side on our backs as we stared up at the ceiling. I put him through his paces this morning and neither of us could yet draw breath to speak.

After several minutes, I felt the mattress shift as Adrien rolled on his side to face me. I turned my head to meet his gaze and we shared a shy, private smile before he spoke.

Running his fingertips over my wrist, he studied my tattoo, "This still amazes me."

I fought the urge to pull my arm away, because he was tickling me, and replied, "Why for?"

He paused in his torment to press a kiss at the center of the gardenia, brushing the tip of his nose against my sensitive skin before looking at me once more, "That in a small way you've kept me with you."

I looked away as the flush of embarrassment crept up my neck into my cheeks.

He shook me gently, "What is it?"

I flipped onto my side and focused on his forearm where my nightingale rested. "It's just that...when I got it, it was more of a wounded reminder to keep from getting hurt again. Of course, the context has changed quite a bit recently..."

Adrien trailed soft kisses over my forehead and nose until I looked him in the eyes, "You will never know the depths of my sorrow and guilt, Luce. But I will work every day for the rest of our lives to prove I'm worthy of you."

I felt tears well up at his fervent promise and I kissed him, "That could be a very long time, Aydo."

"Hope so." He grinned against my mouth.

* * *

"You've got that faraway look again," Nova's voice broke through my daydream.

"Sorry. Just thinking about...*stuff*."

"You owe me details, you know. Starting with why you haven't worn your own pajamas in weeks..."

I laughed, blushing at the recollection, "Well, you remember that first night I spent with Adrien when Rhys came to surprise you?"

"Yeah..."

"Well, I wasn't lying when I said we didn't have sex." I shook my head and covered my face with my hands.

"Oh, come on, Stel...I've told you about Rhys pretending to run in slow-motion wearing nothing but his Keen sandals. Whatever you have to say can't be *that* awkward. He still hasn't forgiven me for sharing that little morsel..." Nova bit the corner of her lip and quirked an eyebrow at me.

I let out a heavy, put-upon sigh, "And you're reminding me of that brain-bleach-worthy moment again?! Sheesh!"

When she elbowed me, I caved, "Fine, I'll tell you. We were making out and I was wearing my shirt and jammies. We got really into it and sort of...basically...*dry-humped*..." I trailed off, staring up at the flight attendant call button.

Hazarding a glance from the corner of my eye, I saw Nova's face completely devoid of expression, save for saucer-wide, blue eyes.

And then the laughter began. She laughed so hard she began to wheeze, her shoulders shaking while no sounds came out.

Frustrated, I glared at her until she stopped having a seizure, "Are you quite finished?"

"So, basically, you guys—" she swallowed a chortle and whispered, "*dry-humped*...and he, you know, on your pajama pants?!"

I slumped, glowering at my dearest friend in the world, "Yes, you wretched human!"

She tucked her lips in and smiled at me, knowing I couldn't resist her cartoon-grin face for long.

Not many minutes passed until we were both snickering like two middle school children as our plane touched down in Santa Fe.

* * *

I looked around the dressing room at our tour family and sighed with contentment. While we were close, shared every meal, and went on little adventures together, we still had our own microcosms which were clearly defined in each corner of the room. The murmur of private conversations, the odd giggle, or a quick lick of music all blended together into a soothing background as Nova and I sat in front of the mirrors and applied our makeup for the evening's show.

I had to admit, however, it felt very strange not to share this space with *Loft*. They had been our tour companions for so many shows; their absence left a definite void.

I had to admit even more, though, that I really just missed Adrien. Keenly.

* * *

Boulder, one week ago.

"So how did you get here?" Adrien asked as he poked around the various pots of glitter and makeup spread out over the desk in our hotel room.

I thought for a moment I should be coy, but I knew what he meant.

Snapping the lid closed on my lipstick, "A combination of factors, really."

"How so? I mean...you're in the entertainment industry, but you planned on theatre and opera in college. How did you end up being a belly dancer of all things?" His voice held no judgment or scorn— lucky for him. "Don't look at me like that, Luce...I'm in awe of you and Nova. It's just not something that was ever on your radar. We used to dance together, but...I don't know, I'm just curious how and when your path changed."

Adrien opened a small jar and dipped in his pinky finger. When he lifted it out, his fingertip was coated in a layer of antique gold which he then brought towards my lips.

Smiling, I held still as he pressed the pad of his digit against the center of my full bottom lip, leaving a shimmer of glitter behind.

"You have been paying attention..." I murmured with a grin and gave his thigh a squeeze.

He leaned forward and brushed a kiss over my forehead before returning to his role as makeup assistant. When he found my iridescent, Swarovski bejeweled bindi, he dabbed spirit gum on the back and placed it where his lips had just been.

"I could get used to this, Aydo."

He chuckled, "You're stalling...tell how me how Stel came to be."

I sighed, picking up my false eyelashes to apply the glue, "Well, you and I had big plans once upon a time."

He didn't respond, but I heard his breath catch. When I hazarded a glance his way, Adrien's face had gone white.

Turning towards him, I cupped his face with my free hand, "I'm not trying to make you feel bad, love, but if you want me to answer your questions, you have to hear the whole story."

He dropped his head, chin to chest, for a moment. When he met my eyes once more, he smiled weakly, "I'll never stop feeling guilty, Luce. Please continue."

I faced the mirror and placed the lashes on my right eyelid, "After things...ended, shall we way, I had to make some fast decisions. I switched my college plans from USC to University of Washington, which was my dad's alma mater. He was already moving back to Seattle when we were supposed to be taking off for California, so I figured sticking close to him would be better for me. When I started in the fall, I introduced myself as Stel or Stella and it stuck."

"So, you still got your BFA?" Adrien queried.

I placed my left set of lashes, "Yes; I majored in theatre, minored in opera and dance. The second minor came later. There was this awesome Lebanese restaurant near my dorm and we would eat there almost every week. On some nights they would have live belly dancers but, you know, the more traditional kind. I got to be friends with one of the girls who was Lebanese and had grown up dancing with her mom and aunts. Her name was Faya. She was also a student at the University and after hanging out for several months and going to various clubs, she convinced me that I should let her and her mom teach me their ways. Her mom actually ran a small, but relatively successful studio and I let her drag me to a rehearsal on a Sunday afternoon. I picked it up quickly, joined their troupe, and started filling in for Faya and the others at the restaurant."

"So, how did you become Candéo?" Adrien began handing me my tools to style my hair.

My eyes misted with happiness as I reflected on those days that changed the path of my life.

* * *

Seattle, five years ago.

"Come on, Stel, we need to get to our seats." Faya urged as we picked our way through the aisles of the auditorium.

We had spent all our tip money on really great seats to see the Belly Supreme Dance Stars who had come through Seattle on their national tour. I had no idea who half of these people were, but Faya was beside herself.

As the show began with a massive group number, my eyes were dazzled by the glitter, sequins and metallic Wings of Isis, until the music took a dark and mysterious turn, revealing six, stunning...what were they?

"Faya," I slapped her arm, "Who are those dancers?"

She was staring at the traditional Oriental performers, so I had to nudge her a few times before she answered me, "Hm? Oh, they are the Tribal Fusion dancers," she answered dismissively.

The rest of the evening, I felt myself light up every time one of them graced the stage with their slinky, serpentine movements punctuated by mind-boggling pops and locks.

I was utterly smitten.

* * *

"I grew restless with the traditional troupe and by that time, Nova had joined. We had gravitated towards each other almost immediately, often

getting paired up because we had this natural synchronicity that made dancing with her seamless and easy. We started to sneak off and take classes with other dance instructors...Tribal teachers, specifically. We went through a certification process to get our teaching credits, started choreographing our own stuff, and broke away from Faya and her mom's troupe. They were actually pretty upset and it was a while before Faya would even talk to us. We started traveling around, taking workshops, teaching, and performing. That's how we started meeting and making friends with all of the folks with us here on the tour. We became a family. Nova and I opened our own studio a couple years ago in Portland and all of our family pays us a little rent to teach their classes there, too."

Adrien was not making any sounds, so I peeked at him out of the corner of my eye. He studied me.

"What?" I asked self-consciously as I slid the last hairpin home.

"You. You're amazing." Uncaring of my lipstick—we had to work on that—he leaned in and kissed me deeply, speeding up my pulse and raising goose bumps all over my skin.

Breathless, I laughed, "Damn, Aydo. That mouth needs to be registered as a lethal weapon."

"I love you." He said simply.

I beamed.

* * *

"Fuuuuhhh!" Nova groaned in frustration and broke my reverie.

I paused in the middle of a mascara sweep, "What's wrong?"

"Fucking eyelashes are *not* cooperating tonight! Look!" She turned and pointed angrily at the smear of black lash glue on her eyelid.

I stuck out my bottom lip, pouting in sympathy, "Just let it dry completely, pull off the glue, touch up your eye shadow, and start again. We've plenty of time."

She grumbled unintelligibly, and then, "I know, it's just annoying."

My phone chimed and I scrabbled to grab it so quickly, I knocked over my chair which made everyone laugh at me. I didn't care, though, and answered the call as I slipped out into the hallway.

"Aydo." I breathed, "I was just thinking about you."

"Luce, thank the gods you picked up. I miss you." His voice was a soothing rumble in my ear.

"I miss you, too. This is our last show in New Mexico, and then we're onto Nevada. How are you?" I glanced at the clock on the wall to make sure I didn't run out of time.

"Want to meet up in Vegas and get hitched?" He teased.

I sighed heavily, "No, love. I'll see you in Portland before you know it, then you can see my dad, meet my step-mom, and my fur balls."

Adrien growled in exasperation, "I...I..."

"What, Aydo? What's wrong?" He sounded miserable and my heart twisted.

"I *ache* for you, Luce. I *crave* you. I haven't slept at all since we parted in Colorado." His tone was desolate and fraught with even more unspoken things.

I could completely relate, except for the not sleeping part. I had been able to sleep; I just missed his warmth lying next to me.

"Aydo, it's going to be okay. I love you. Thank you for calling me; I needed to hear you."

I heard his deep breath on the line as he got himself under control, "I love you most. I'll talk to you tomorrow. Kill it, tonight."

"Bye, love."

We hung up and I slunk back into the dressing room to finish getting ready.

My phone went off again just as I came in the door and I smiled and answered, "Just couldn't wait, could you?"

No one spoke; I only heard agitated breathing. Then they hung up.

I frowned at the screen, but the number showed up as 'blocked'.

Probably a wrong number.

14

Vegas.

I stared out the hotel window at the Strip below, mesmerized by the lights.

I hadn't spoken to Adrien in days, only getting short text messages that consisted of him missing me, loving me, and others of the filthy variety. There had been a couple more hang up calls, too.

"You have to stop moping, Stel. It's not like he hasn't been calling only to just miss you." Nova spoke from the bathroom doorway.

I looked at her mournfully over my shoulder and sighed, "I know. I just..."

She rolled her eyes, "Seriously, Stel. I haven't seen my *husband* in over a month. *Husband.*"

I ran to my friend and hugged her, "I'm so sorry! I'm being a completely self-centered turd-nugget! I lub yew, Vava. Forgive me, pweeeease?"

She worked her hand up to palm my face and shoved me—gently—away, "Stahp! Of course I do. You just needed a wakeup call. So—" She turned back towards the bathroom mirror to check her eye makeup, "I know we don't normally do this, but I think we should go out and enjoy a little bit of Vegas. What say you?"

I grinned, "Let me get changed!"

Ten minutes later, I was tastefully dressed in a deep teal maxi dress and my favorite hemp wedges with my waves of mahogany and purple-streaked hair pinned up loosely.

Nova braided her long brown hair to the side, showing off the shaved side of her head. She had slipped on an empire-waist sundress in a soft grey that accentuated her curves, and a pair of black, roman-style sandals.

The men of Las Vegas are in big trouble, I thought wryly as we linked arms and made our way down into the throng of sin.

* * *

We didn't bother with the casinos, but contented ourselves by simply walking around and taking in all the *very* interesting sights and people.

I spotted a swanky-looking sushi restaurant and dragged Nova into it where we lucked out and got seated quickly.

Unfortunately, we were placed by a rowdy group of men at the table next to us, but I was determined to eat delicious food and have a ridiculously overpriced cocktail.

I sat back, sipping something called a Pink Thruster—it was the dirty name that drew me in—and really, it just tasted like a very strong Cosmo.

"I'm glad we did this," I held out my pink drink to toast Nova's iced tea—*not* of the Long Island variety.

"Me too," She clinked her glass against mine and let her eyes roam around the dining room of the restaurant. "I never thought I would say this, but compared to some of these folks, we look like June Cleaver."

I giggled, "I know!" I gestured with my eyes for her to look at yet another breast-augmented *lady* with collagen-injected everything stuffed into a lime-green mini dress. I couldn't imagine someone like that click-clacking around the streets of Portland.

We ordered an array of rolls and sashimi items, continuing to enjoy our friend-time and people watching.

Someone bumped into my seat, causing me to drop a spicy tuna roll in my lap and getting wasabi all over my dress.

"What the fuck?!" I turned toward the offender.

"I'm so sorry!" The man grabbed a napkin and tried to help clean me up.

I grabbed his wrists, "Not so fast—*Christian*?!"

Familiar brown eyes looked up at me and he smiled, "Holy shit...Luce MacLean!" He scooped me up out of my seat and hugged me, my feet dangling above the floor.

"Uh....down, please?" He released me and I patted him awkwardly on the chest.

"Sorry, I've been drinking a little. Makes me affectionate." He grinned sheepishly.

"Christian, this is my best friend, Nova." I made the introduction quickly when I noticed my friend's wide-eyed expression. *Prom Christian?* She mouthed and I gave her a subtle nod.

They shook hands and he sat down at my gestured invitation.

"I'm in shock at running into you here of all places. How have you been? What are you doing? Are you single?" Christian's eye twinkled with humor even as he interrogated me.

I tilted my head as I regarded his handsome face. He really hadn't changed that much from the way I remembered him. He was still built very well, with a ready smile, and a natural charm. It reminded me why it had been so easy for me to decide to drag him to bed for my first time.

"Well, I'm *not* single. I'm great and having a lovely dinner with my best friend. We've been on a tour all summer, performing in cities across America." I wanted to get his last question answered immediately so I could set the boundaries.

As it turned out, Christian was in Vegas with some friends for a bachelor weekend. He was a college football coach back in his home state of Indiana.

He lingered only a short while longer before excusing himself to return to his friends—the rowdy bunch at the next table—and apologizing again for causing me to drop my food.

* * *

After we finished up our late dinner, and I managed to clean the wasabi off with my napkin and some water, Nova and I left the restaurant and headed in the direction of our hotel.

"We don't even have stories of debauchery to tell our grandkids, Vava," I pouted.

She snorted, "Let's face it, Stel, we're not the debauchery type. It's not a bad thing to be a good girl, you know."

I sighed, "Yeah, I guess."

We both stopped and turned at the sound of a man calling my name. *Christian.*

He was barely out of breath even though it was apparent he had sprinted after us, "I thought maybe we could have breakfast before you leave Vegas."

I smiled and patted him on the cheek, "Maybe. Depends on if I'm up early enough. We have to be to the airport by one."

"Here, take my card. It has my cell on it so you can give me a call if you can make it." He pulled me into a hug and I'm pretty sure he sniffed me.

I allowed the embrace to happen, enjoying the familiarity and the solidness of Christian's body against mine. But after a moment, I pulled away. It felt wrong and weird.

"Good to see you, Christian." My cheeks heated a bit and I had to look away when I saw his tired eyes and soft grin. He'd looked at me much the same way at the end of our one night together and I did *not* want to think about how adorable he still was. I already felt awkward enough.

"You too, Luce. Nova, great to meet you again." He stuffed his hands in his suit pants pockets and walked in the direction he'd run from.

She waved at his retreating back and gave me a loaded look. After the hugging scene with Christian, Nova was acting strange—stranger than usual.

"What is it? Why are you looking at me like that?" I stood in front of the revolving door that led to the lobby of our hotel.

She opened her mouth to speak, thought better of it, and shoved me through the entrance.

I froze just inside, getting knocked in the back by the edge of the door, and was propelled forward into Adrien's waiting arms.

"Aydo!" I squeaked, clinging to him for dear life.

He righted me, tucking an escaped tendril of hair behind my ear.

"Hey, little songbird." His voice was a just above murmur and heavy with exhaustion.

"Surpriiiise." Nova spoke from behind me.

I turned and pointed at her, "Sneaky wench!"

"You're welcome." She grinned cheekily at me, then said to Adrien, "I had her stuff moved into your room while we were out. Have a good night, you two."

"Come on, love," he laced his fingers with mine and we boarded the elevator.

* * *

I was still stunned, but that didn't stop me from attacking Adrien the second we shut our door. I cupped his face and tried to kiss him, but he leaned away and trapped my hands against his chest.

"You smell different."

Fuck! I thought anxiously. I probably smelled like Christian's cologne.

He didn't wait for an answer, instead following up with, "And who was that guy all over you outside?"

I bounced with impatience and whined, "Can't we talk about this later? I *missed* you."

His dusky brows arched over his troubled green eyes.

I sighed, "Fine." Taking my hands back from him, I kicked off my shoes, padded over to the king-sized bed and sat down, patting the spot next to me.

He obliged, removing his own sneakers before joining me.

"That man was Christian—as in the guy that took me to prom. He just so happened to be in town for a friend's bachelor party and we ran into each other at dinner. He gave me a hug goodbye, which is probably why I smell funny." I gave him a look when I was finished as if to ask, *Satisfied?*

"It just didn't look right from where I was standing." He rubbed his hands over his face.

"I can understand that, but you have nothing to worry about, Aydo. I'm *all* yours." I leaned forward and tried to kiss him, but he retreated again.

In a show of possession and overt masculinity I had never seen before, Adrien pushed me flat against the mattress and covered my body with his, claiming my lips almost violently as he ground the swelling ridge of his shaft against my rapidly heating core.

Hot damn! I met the thrusts of his tongue with wild abandon, gasping in delight as he dragged his mouth down my jaw and throat, scratching me with the shadowy beard on his face.

In a shock of pleasure and a little pain, he bit down into the flesh of my trapezius and whispered, "*Mine.*"

I could only nod as passion and arousal consumed me and I pulled at his clothes.

"Uh-uh, little songbird," He stood up, looming over my prone form, "I'm the boss right now. My clothes come off when I'm ready. Can you handle that?"

I was distracted from the question, because he was skimming his hands up my legs and fast-approaching my panties, but he suddenly flipped me over and smacked my ass.

"Hey!" I glared at him over my shoulder.

"I asked if you could handle me being the boss tonight." His voice had turned velvety but with a slight edge.

"Yes, damn it!"

He rewarded me with a dark smile before continuing his exploration, pressing his fingers into my tight IT bands and massaging my rump before he rolled me onto my back again, slipped my vibrant purple, lace boy shorts off, and dropped them on the floor.

My dress was bunched around my waist as Adrien settled between my thighs, resting one forearm over my hips to hold me still. His breath was a warm caress against my sex before I nearly convulsed at the long swipe of his tongue.

"Oh, god!" I squirmed, but I was his captive. His sexy chuckle vibrated against my clit and my eyes rolled back in my head.

He loved me thoroughly, slipping a finger inside, coaxing and persuading my body until I came with a whimper, gasping and clutching my fingers in his hair.

Placing kisses on each of my hip bones and delving his tongue into my navel, Adrien worked his way up, removing my dress in the process until I was pinned beneath him once more.

We laid there quietly, studying the contours of each other's face. He nuzzled me, just barely touching his lips to mine before he lifted his head to search my eyes.

"I love you." He breathed.

I blinked up at him in a slow and feline fashion, the hint of smile just beginning to shine.

"I so very much love you, Aydo."

He sat up, still kneeling between my knees, and leisurely removed his clothes, his eyes never leaving mine.

When he was at last gloriously nude and draped over me once more, he sealed his lips over mine, taunting and teasing me with his tongue and nips from his teeth.

My fever for him climbed and I arched into his groping hands, moaning when he lifted my hips and sheathed himself with one, swift plunge.

He sat back on his knees, gripping my hips to push and pull me back and forth in a deliberate and torturous rhythm that made me cry out from the intensity of the angle.

My breath became labored and as I gazed up at Adrien, I could see his eyes fixed on my face as he bit his bottom lip. Every muscle he possessed stood out as he used his strength to piston my slick channel around his steely shaft.

"Aydo..." I murmured.

"Come for me, Luce..." He hissed through his gritted teeth. He was barely hanging on.

My back bowed off the bed as I shattered in his arms, sobbing as my climax overtook me.

Adrien folded over, moaning against my breasts as his own release followed. I felt the hot jets of his seed filling me up and I reveled in it.

Coated in sweat, we curled up under the covers. I had a leg and arm across Adrien's torso with my chin on his shoulder, my head sharing his pillow.

I feathered kisses all over his face where I could reach and he laughed quietly, turning his face to capture my lips in a slow, sweet kiss.

"I like it when you're the boss." I spoke low in his ear.

His laugh grew and mine joined in until we were in tears.

All tangled up, we fell into a blissful and sated slumber.

* * *

I watched Adrien from the bed the next morning as he stuffed his backpack, preparing to leave.

"This sucks."

He paused, "I know, but it's almost over." He sat down next to me, taking my hand between his.

"Aydo, what happens after the tours are over? We haven't talked about any of that. I live in Portland and you live in San Diego."

He kissed my palm, causing a tingle to run up my arm.

"Well, you own your house, right?" He bit the pad of my thumb and I gasped.

"Yes, but what does—?"

"I just rent a place with the guys and our lease is up soon. I figured I would relocate to Portland. Actually, the guys and I have been talking about moving anyway...we can easily do what we do there as well as San Diego. Does that clear things up for you?" He held my palm against his cheek and gazed at me.

My eyes misted a little, "Yes." I leaned in to brush my lips against his, but pulled back, "Just so we're clear: *you* can move in with me, but the boys are on their own."

He chuckled and sucked on my lower lip, "Deal."

15

Seattle was a favorite of ours and the shows had gone amazingly well. We spent hours talking and mingling with members of the audience, taking photos, and even signing some autographs. It was abundantly clear that here on the west coast there was more of a celebrity element where we and our dance family were concerned.

I had been keeping tabs on our Facebook and *Loft's*, making sure to keep our online presence active, but also watching for any kind of shady activity of the Tabitha variety. Adrien assured me that he was checking as well and had not seen much more outside of what we'd already discussed.

Personally, I was more concerned at her lack of action. To me that meant she was scheming and plotting something. I was fairly certain that the hang up calls had been her, but without a number to tie to them, I had no proof.

The familiar pangs of jealousy and insecurity flared as I skimmed through photos on the *Loft* page and saw girls hanging all over Adrien and the rest of the guys. I had to breathe deeply and remind myself that I deal with fans that like to get a little too much in my personal space also. It's a fine line that artists walk, because you don't want to offend people by shoving them away or telling them to fuck off.

I sighed, forcing myself to look at all of the pictures and confront my demons directly. I knew Adrien almost better than I knew myself and I read the discomfort in his body language in every image.

Picking up my phone, I texted him:

> **-I love you, Aydo.**

He fired back almost immediately:

> **-Ooh, I like this game. I love you, too, little songbird.**
>
> **-Let me guess...you've been on Facebook.**

Fuck! I looked around my hotel room for a hidden camera.

> **-How in the *hell* did you know that?!**

He responded:

> **-Lol, I didn't. You just told me...are you excited to see me tomorrow?**

I dialed his number and he answered on the first ring, "Well, I *was* excited, but then you were a dick..."

"Hey, now! Leave him out of this." I could hear the cheerfulness in his voice.

I shook my head, "I admit I was on the page for *Loft* and I saw all the slut-puppies pawing all over you and the guys. I didn't like it, but I worked through it. I could read your body language well enough to see you weren't enjoying yourself, although they probably thought you were."

"Yeah. I used to think the girls would be an awesome perk, but quickly realized how hollow it all was. None of them were you." He spoke softly and I heard the rustling of sheets in the background.

"Awwww! You're so sweet, Aydo!" I teased him in a childlike voice.

"Hush, woman. Better get your rest, because tomorrow I am going to be chasing your naked ass until you're panting and spent."

My inner muscles clenched at the promise he whispered.

"Mmmm, that sounds promising. Goodnight, love." I murmured.

"Goodnight. I love you."

* * *

Rhys picked us up at the airport in Portland and we made plans with the rest of the group to meet at the venue early the next day.

Nova and Rhys lived right across the street from me and we had our own studio space in the separate garage behind my house. I hugged them both and made my way up the path to my front porch, but the door swung open before I could get out my key.

"Daddy!" I quickly dropped everything as my father swept me off of the ground into a bear hug.

I breathed in his comforting scent of sandalwood and fresh laundry, feeling like a little girl again for a moment.

Dad set me back on my feet and held my face in his large, paw-like hands. He inspected me closely before nodding to himself as if to confirm his assessment of my person. He grabbed my bags and I followed him inside.

"You're a weirdo, Daddy-o." I kicked my shoes off on the foyer rug, sighing in contentment to be in my own cave again.

The scrabble of claws preceded the onslaught of my furry children, Edgar and Mata.

My fluffy Maine Coon tabby, Mata, purred and rubbed her body all over me while I crouched and hugged Edgar, my blue pit bull. Feeling their unconditional love brought tears to my eyes.

"Thanks for taking care of things for me," I stood and hugged my dad again.

"Of course, kiddo. Anything for you." With his arm still around me, we walked to the back of the house into the kitchen where Alice was cooking something that smelled heavenly.

"Hello, Lustella." My stepmother paused in her stirring to come and hug me. She was tiny, so her head tucked under my chin. She still managed to provide more maternal comfort than my own mother within her diminutive stature, though.

"I forget how short you are, Alice." I teased.

She released me and swatted my bottom with the towel she'd draped over her shoulder, "That's enough sass, or you're not getting any dinner."

I grinned cheekily at her and scooped Mata into my arms, nuzzling and scratching her favorite spot under her chin. She gave me an Eskimo kiss and scent-marked my cheek before squirming away to ravish her food dish.

Edgar, however, pressed his warm and muscular self against my thigh, panting happily and smiling up at me as only a pit bull can smile. I rubbed his soft, un-docked ears and leaned down to kiss his forehead.

Dad carried my things up to my room and I trailed up the stairs after him.

"When do you want to talk, Daddy?" I asked from my bedroom doorway.

"Maybe over dinner, if that's okay. Are you fine with Alice hearing it?" He stood before me, rubbing my upper arms.

"Yes, of course. I'm going to just take a little time to get a shower and change into some fresh clothes, and then I'll join you both. I stashed a bottle of South African Syrah behind the cereal in the pantry if you want to decant it for us to have with dinner." I gave him an affectionate squeeze around the waist.

"Clever girl; I didn't think to look there. I'll have a glass waiting for you." He kissed the top of my head and left my room, closing the door behind him.

I shut my eyes and took several deep, cleansing breaths. It was almost like the night I ended up staying in Adrien's room, the feeling of being a little overwhelmed. I flopped onto my bed. *Oh, I missed you, too,* I thought as I rolled back and forth on my king-sized memory foam mattress. Hotels are great and have wonderful pillows, but my bed? My bed is fucking awesome. I liked to save money where I could, but I invested in a high-quality bed with high thread count sheets and bedding. Adrien was going to love it.

Oops, I thought. I was supposed to call him when I landed. I sent him a quick text instead.

-Call in you in a few, just got home and need a shower.

I stepped into my en suite and turned on the water in my large, glassed-in shower. Stripping out of my traveling clothes, I stood under the warm spray and felt the months of the tour rinse down the drain.

Washed and dried, I put on a sports bra, yoga pants, a hoodie, and slippers before grabbing my phone and heading back downstairs to claim my glass of wine.

I glanced at the screen and saw that Adrien had not answered my text. I didn't expect him to, because I said I would call him, but I was used to him responding even when he didn't need to.

I sauntered into the kitchen and snatched the waiting glass off of the kitchen island, "Do I still have a few minutes? I was supposed to call Adrien when I landed."

Alice and my dad glanced up at me from the stove where they'd been speaking quietly, "Yes, of course. You've got about twenty minutes."

"Thanks, Alice." I went back upstairs to my room and leaned against the headboard of my bed as I made my call.

It went straight to voicemail.

Frowning, I tried again with the same result.

-Aydo, will you please call me when you can? Your phone is going to voicemail when I call. Wtf?

I took a sip of my wine and nearly moaned. I hadn't had a decent glass of wine since before I'd left on tour. I was just happy my dad hadn't found this bottle while I was gone.

My phone buzzed and I picked it up.

-Adrien is busy right now, who is this?

I felt the bottom drop out of my stomach as the hairs on the back of my neck prickled. Something was very wrong.

I decided not to respond, because clearly someone else had possession of Adrien's phone and I had a sneaking suspicion on exactly who that person was. Although how she knew how to find him I wasn't sure just yet.

I wanted to call Nova, but I knew that she and Rhys were probably in the midst of an enthusiastic reunion—I wasn't one to clam-jam a friend. I drained my wine glass, fortifying my nerves, and joined my dad and step-mom once more.

We settled at my vintage farm table and dined on homemade spaghetti with tons of vegetables mixed in rather than meat. I hummed happily as I ate the heavenly sauce Alice had made from scratch. The woman could cook and had taught me most of what I knew in a short amount of time.

"So, Lustella," my dad began, "if you're ready to fill us in, we are all ears."

I took another large sip of wine and two healthy bites of my pasta before I spoke, "Here it goes..."

* * *

I finished my story and had to laugh a little at the stunned expressions on my dad and Alice's faces.

Dad shook his head, "Wow. That poor boy...I had no idea that his parents were so neglectful. He was prime pickings for a sick individual like that girl."

I nodded sadly, "Yeah, and what's more...she's still around."

"What?!" This outburst came from Alice, surprisingly. She never raised her voice.

"In her mind, I ruined everything for her and now she she's seen that Adrien and I are back together, it's like she has snapped again." I folded my hands over my over-stuffed stomach.

My dad wiped his mouth and shook his head again, "You think she's here in Portland?"

I told them about the postings online, the hang-up calls I had received, and the text message from Adrien's phone earlier.

"I think we should go to the hotel where the band is staying," my dad announced. He rose and started clearing the dishes from the table.

I looked to Alice for guidance, but she simply nodded, "You're right, Malcolm. We need to be proactive about this."

What the...? I sat there in shock while my parents cleaned my kitchen and gathered me up to depart the house and head downtown to *Loft's* hotel.

* * *

I tried calling again as we entered the lobby, but it continued to go straight to voicemail. I had a sinking feeling in my stomach that something bad was either about to happen, or was happening already. My palms were sweaty as I approached the front desk.

"Hi there," I put on my most winning smile as I greeted the young man behind the counter.

He blinked at me, a bit dazed by the full force of my charm, before he responded. "Hello, Miss, how may I be of assistance?"

"My name is Luce MacLean and my boyfriend Adrien O'Rourke booked us a room for this weekend."

His friendly expression faltered slightly when I mentioned the b-word, but he dutifully began typing something into his computer while I glanced nervously over my shoulder at my parents.

My dad was looking very intimidating as he stood with his arms crossed, taking note of everyone and everything in the room. Alice had her hand tucked into the crook of his elbow and gave me a gentle smile of encouragement.

"Did you lose your key already, Miss MacLean?" The young man asked.

I cocked my head in confusion...*already?*

My phone pinged and I glanced down to see Toko's name on the screen.

Duh! I thought. Why didn't I just try one of the guys when I couldn't get through?

"Excuse me, I have to take this." I turned on my heel and walked a short distance away to answer Toko's call.

"Luce?" He didn't wait for me to answer when I hit the button.

"I'm here, T, what's wrong?" He sounded panicked.

"Have you talked to Adrien?" He asked.

My stomach bottomed-out completely, "Actually, no. I haven't been able to get a hold of him for a couple of hours. It goes straight to voicemail when I call and when I tried sending him a text, someone else responded. Did you all check in together?"

"Yeah, then he went into his room and we haven't seen him since. We didn't know what to think though when we heard yelling and thumping. I thought for a minute you came early and were...you know. But the more it went on, the more we realized it wasn't what we thought. I'm worried, Luce."

"I'm in the lobby with my father and step-mom, what floor are you on? We'll come up and figure this out right now." My spine had hardened and I felt the fire of vengeance flaring to life throughout my body.

If Tabitha was here and she had done something to Adrien, there would be blood.

After Toko told me their floor number, I boarded the elevator with my parents.

I sent a quick text to Nova to let her know what was happening, but that I wanted her to stay put.

When we exited into the hallway, Dad and Alice flanked me as I walked with a dark purpose towards Toko, Kyle, and Andy.

I made quick introductions, then they pointed towards the door that separated us from Adrien and, if my intuition was correct, Tabitha.

I could hear yelling, but the sound-proofing in this hotel was very high-quality so I couldn't discern specific words. What I *could* tell is that it was only one voice doing the yelling, and *she* sounded like a lunatic.

I felt my resolve falter and I turned towards my father, "Daddy, what do I do?"

His light eyes softened as he gazed down at me, "Fight, kiddo. I'm right here with you."

I raised my fist and pounded on the solid wood and the screeching stopped. I moved away from the peephole and my small army did the same.

"Who is it?" I heard *fucking Tabitha* ask just on the other side.

My father spoke up then, "Hotel security, Ma'am. We have had several noise complaints about shouting and loud noises coming from this room and we're here to make sure everyone is okay."

She was silent for a beat, "We're fine! No need to trouble yourselves. You can go now."

I shared a tacit look with my father and he nodded.

Without another moment's hesitation, I took a deep breath and front-kicked the door open, knocking Tabitha onto the floor in the process.

I could only gloat about my martial arts prowess for a beat before Tabitha was flying at me.

"You! You've ruined everything!" She shoved me once and was moving forward to do it again, so I stepped to the outside of her body, redirected her outstretched arms, and raised my other hand to strike her in the throat as I moved away. She fell to the ground, clutching her neck as she tried to breathe. Her eyes were murderous as she glared up at me.

I shrugged at her, "Hapkido, bitch."

I scanned the room, which had been completely destroyed by Tabitha's rage. The bedding was all over the floor, pillows ripped open, a lamp and other things that had been on top of the desk were scattered about. I suspected that if the TV hadn't been bolted to the wall, she would have thrown that, too.

The bathroom door was shut and when I tried the knob, I found it was locked. I rapped my knuckles against it, "Aydo?"

I held my breath until the door finally creaked open and Adrien poked his head out. He looked shell-shocked and had a hand-shaped welt on one side of his face. There was a little blood trickling from his nose as well.

When he saw me, he sagged against the door frame in relief before stumbling into my arms.

"Thank the gods, Luce. Oh, thank you. I love you. I'm so glad you're here." He clutched me against his chest, kissing my hair and murmuring nonsense.

I glanced at the gathering in the hallway and smiled.

"Dad! Where did you get a zip-tie?" I demanded when I saw he had bound Tabitha's wrists.

He smirked and shrugged. Once a Secret Service guy, always a Secret Service guy...

* * *

My father tried to convince Adrien to press charges against Tabitha for assault, but he refused. The hotel was already going to file charges for the property damage she had inflicted on the hotel room. He thought that was punishment enough.

I was torn between what I thought he should do and my own vengeful feelings. I knew that his reasons for not pressing charges were born out of pity for her, but at the same time my sympathy for a person only goes so far.

The manager comped the rooms, because it was their error in not checking Tabitha's identification when she came in and pretended to be me in order to get a room key. Neither Adrien nor the boys wanted to stay there anymore, however. Consequently, my house was going to be very full.

Kyle, Toko, and Andy loaded up their rented van and followed my dad's shiny, black SUV back to my home.

When we got out, Nova came running across the street with her arms crossed over her breasts to keep them still. I laughed as she caught me in a hug, "Control your tatas, Vava!"

She slapped my arm, and then turned to hug Adrien, too. "Are you guys okay? What happened?"

"Hey Alice?" I called to her from the sidewalk.

"Yeah, honey?" She paused by my front door.

"You have more spaghetti?"

* * *

Rhys, Nova, Kyle, Toko, Andy, Adrien, my parents, and I sat around my living room with plates of pasta in our laps. What? Dealing with psycho bitches makes me peckish.

I let Adrien tell the rest of the group what had happened, since I didn't know the full story myself. Apparently, Tabitha had figured out that my home base was Portland and thought that it would be the best place for her to make her move.

She lied to the person at the front desk of the hotel so she could get a key, and then let herself into Adrien's room. He had thought I was there to surprise him early, but caught on quickly as soon as he turned around to see Tabitha standing there.

When she made a move to come onto him, he said he tried to politely reject her and asked her to leave, but that's when she became unglued and hit him across the face. Rather than lay hands on her, he locked himself in the bathroom.

"That was smart thinking to avoid touching her in any way, Adrien." This was from my dad.

"Thank you, Sir. I know from past experience with her that she will use anything at her disposal to ruin people and I knew that if I even pushed her gently, she would find some way to make it look like I attacked her." He sat his plate on my coffee table and leaned forward, his arms braced on his knees.

I rubbed soothing circles on his back and he smiled weakly at me.

"What is it, Aydo?" I asked, pressing a kiss against his shoulder.

"I feel like a—pardon my language—but, I feel like a total pussy right now, because I ran away and hid from a girl. My own girlfriend had to fly in and rescue me." He leaned back, sinking into my plush leather sofa.

The whole room chuckled, but my father was the one that spoke, "Son, choosing the non-violent path is nothing to be ashamed of."

"Besides, baby, I kind of like the idea of playing your knight in shining armor." I winked and gently elbowed him.

He sighed, but it was with a rueful grin, "So, what exactly did you *do* to her, Luce?"

I looked away, feigning ignorance, "I don't know what you're talking about."

Kyle chimed in, "Dude, it was so badass! First, she went all Bruce Lee and kicked the door in, and then when Tabitha came at her, she hit her in the throat! It was the coolest thing I've ever seen. Totally hot, Luce—" He flicked his eyes over to Adrien, "Sorry, dude. Woman's got mad skills."

Adrien looked at me with renewed admiration, "I'm sorry I missed it."

I shrugged it off and exchanged a smirk with my dad. After all, he was the one who taught me everything I knew.

Nova piped up then, "Well, it's getting late and we've got quite a big day tomorrow. We'll head back across the street and let you all settle in and get some rest." With a quick hug for my parents, Adrien, and me, they departed.

"We'll clean up the kitchen, Luce." Andy said as he rose and left the room.

"Andy, you really need to shut up. I mean, gosh! I can hardly get a word in edgewise!" I harassed him from my comfortable spot on the sofa.

He peeked around the corner, granting me a small and rare smile, before retreating. Toko and Kyle got up and followed after him.

"Well, kiddo, I think that's our cue. You have everything handled down here?"

I stood and walked into my father's arms, "Yes, thank you so much for everything today."

He kissed the top of my head, "Don't even mention it. Goodnight, sweetheart."

I gave Alice a quick squeeze and they headed upstairs to bed.

"Okay, boys—" I spoke in the doorway of my kitchen, "I have an extra bedroom upstairs that you can flip for, and then these two couches in here are actually pull-outs. There's a full bathroom on this floor and a full bathroom upstairs that you would share with my parents."

The three of them looked at each other and shrugged indecisively before Toko answered for everyone, "I was just going to sleep on that recliner in the corner. I think we'll all just crash down here, if that's okay."

I nodded, "Okay, Aydo and I will get the bedding and stuff. Thank you so much for cleaning the dishes, guys. You didn't have to do that and I really do appreciate it."

They waved me off and I dragged Adrien to the second floor to help me gather sheets, blankets, and pillows for everyone. Edgar's tail thumped happily on the floor when we reached the upstairs landing. My kids were well-behaved and stayed up in my open bedroom when I banished them earlier.

"Soon, honey." I cooed to him as we loaded up with linens and headed back downstairs. I was rewarded with another tail thump and a low chuff.

Adrien and I readied the beds—and recliner—for the guys with very little conversation. I could feel his eyes tracking my every movement, however, and I felt desire and heat begin to build low in my belly. I had a plan forming quickly in my mind of exactly what I planned to do to him once we were in my room.

I gave him a slow, seductive smile and he visibly gulped.

I poked my head into the kitchen once more, "Fellas? You're all set down here, make yourselves at home. We're going to turn in."

All three waved over their shoulders and muttered some form of "good night". I figured I was safe to scoot.

I grabbed Adrien's hand in mine and led him up to my bedroom.

* * *

I kicked out Mata and Edgar—both protested—and closed the door behind them, turning to find Adrien watching me. The moon shone through the gauzy purple curtains, making the angles of his face more prominent.

"I was really worried, Aydo." I stepped towards him.

He pulled off his shirt and I paused to admire the carved lines of his torso. He chuckled softly and I raised my eyes to his, smiling without apology.

I resumed my short path until I stood before him, looking up into the shadows of his gaze.

His breath caught as I dragged my nails up the bumps of his abs to rest my hands on his chest.

"*Really* worried." I whispered against his mouth.

"I know, Luce. I'm sorry, I had no idea she would go that far..." He touched his forehead to mine.

"It's all right now, Aydo. Everything is all right."

He pressed a lingering kiss against my forehead, right over my third eye chakra, and I shivered.

"Thank you for coming after me, little songbird." I felt his smile against my skin.

"Always." I was done with waiting and sealed our lips together, anchoring my fingers in his hair.

With a low groan, Adrien bent and lifted me, turning and laying us on my bed. Sliding down, he lifted the hem of my top and bit my stomach, causing my hips to jerk.

I trapped my bottom lip with my teeth, dimly aware that I had to keep as quiet as possible with my father and stepmother just down the hall.

"Aydo," I gasped.

"What?" He mumbled against my thigh he'd only just exposed.

"We have to be noiseless...my dad has hearing like a wolf." I bit back another cry as his tongue found my center.

He lifted his head and grinned wickedly, "I can be *very* stealthy..." then dropped between my legs again, teasing me with one, long lick before fluttering the tip of his tongue against my clit and slipping his fingers into my moist heat.

I thrashed on the mattress, my head rolling back and forth as he coaxed me into sweet oblivion and I fell apart at his merciless stroking.

He was barely gone from me before I felt his callused hands spread my knees wide and slide home. I nearly came again when he filled me completely. He drew back slowly, thrusting back in hard. Adrien lifted one of my feet so my leg rested against him, my ankle on his shoulder. He pressed his palm flat against my lower abs and I had to clamp my teeth together to keep myself from screaming. When he pushed down, his shaft stroked deliberately against my g-spot and with only a few, deliberate rocks of his hips, my back bowed off the bed and I shoved my fist in my mouth, keening deep in my chest as I seized and shuddered from the magnitude of my release. Adrien's grip tightened towards bruising as he followed me over the edge, setting his teeth against my ankle to silence his raspy moan.

My breathing was labored and I felt boneless as Adrien leaned forward, brushing kisses against my breasts and neck as he sought my mouth. He sucked on my bottom lip as he maneuvered us under the covers, pulling my leg across his waist and tucking my head against his chest.

I was already drifting off when I shook myself awake, "Edgar and Mata, Aydo..."

He was nearly out, too, but he kissed my nose and got up to let them in the bedroom.

Rejoining me underneath the sheets, we cuddled up and my furry children found their spots on the unoccupied sections of my bed.

Utterly spent and exultant, we slept.

17

I woke up the next morning to find my bed empty. Well, aside from Edgar and Mata snoozing happily at the foot of the bed.

I rose and stretched, uncaring that I was naked, before heading into my en suite. There was a sticky note on the mirror from Adrien:

> *Good morning, Love—*
>
> *I couldn't sleep, so I got up early. Didn't want to wake you. I'm out with your dad, but we'll be back soon.*
>
> *I love you.*
>
> *-Aydo*

The line about him being with my dad gave me pause and I frowned, but after a moment's consideration, I figured he was probably safe. *Perhaps he just wanted to give more details about Tabitha and what had happened back in high school?*

I had to shake it off and hope for the best, so I hopped in the shower.

* * *

I dressed in multi-colored patchwork harem pants and a lightweight, white tissue-tee that hung off one shoulder, leaving my hair to air-dry, as I made my way downstairs with Mata draped over my shoulder and Edgar at my heels.

The smell of coffee was irresistible and I stopped to pour a cup before letting Edgar out into my back yard.

After several minutes of enjoying the lush greenery I had cultivated over the last few years, it occurred to me my house was way too quiet. I'd housed a horde of twenty-something men and both of my parents—there should have been murmurs or farting or something making noise.

Slipping back inside, I plopped Mata on her perch by the sliding door and gave Edgar a quick scratch before going to investigate.

The living room was empty and the boys were nowhere to be found.

"Alice? Boys?" I called as I searched every room. Nothing.

The blankets were all folded neatly on the sofas and not a thing was out of place.

I didn't sleep that *late, did I?* I wondered as I went back to the kitchen to check the microwave clock.

It was only ten.

I didn't have to wait much longer, though, because the front door opened and my home was once more filled with sound.

Alice, followed by Kyle, Toko, and Andy came into the kitchen carrying grocery bags.

"Oh, hi, Sweetie!" Alice stopped by my chair to kiss my head.

"You guys went grocery shopping without me?" I pouted.

"Yeah, we wanted to thank you for letting us stay here; Alice was our guide!" Kyle offered cheerfully as he stocked my cupboards and fridge.

I grinned, my heart warm, "You didn't have to do that. But, I thank you."

Toko gave me a wink and Andy actually smiled. His non-descript self was much cuter when he revealed lovely, white teeth.

"Alice, where did Dad take Adrien?" I rose and poured another cup of French roast.

Her eyes twinkled as she answered me, "The gym."

Oh, fuck...

* * *

I checked my phone again and saw it was almost noon. Adrien and my dad had been gone for several hours and, frankly, I was starting to worry.

Alas, there was not much I could do about it, because we all had to meet up at the venue to go over final details for the evening's grand finale show. Tonight we would bring our tour to its conclusion.

I sent Adrien a quick text to let him know we were heading over to the Crystal Ballroom and he needed to get his ass there, pronto.

Just as with the previous nine messages, I received no response. I didn't even get a response from my dad and that *never* happened.

There had to be a very good reason for them both to be ignoring me, but no matter what it was...I intended to take a chunk out of both their asses for making me worry. Jerks.

Nova and Rhys had a fabulous vintage VW bus named Magnolia, which we—the remaining members of *Loft*, Rhys, Nova, and I—piled into so we could meet the rest of our crew at the venue.

***

As Rhys dropped us by the front doors, I saw my dad and Adrien engaged in a seemingly serious conversation out on the sidewalk.

"Hey!" I strode up them, punching them both in the arm.

They jumped and muttered curses while rubbing their abused limbs.

"Where were you guys? I've been trying to get a hold of you both for hours." My hands were on my hips and my toe was a-tapping.

They exchanged a look and my dad answered, "Adrien was up early this morning and I asked if he wanted to tag along with me to the gym. We lost track of time and our phones were in the locker room. Sorry, Honey." He gave me a one-armed hug and kissed the top of my head.

I narrowed my blue eyes that were twins to his, "I call bullshit, *Daddy*. I don't know what you're up to, but I'll find out. Lucky for you I don't have time to sniff it out right now."

Adrien was smirking when I turned my ire on him, "And *you*—" I poked my finger in his chest, "Damn you for making me worry after yesterday's trauma!" Not waiting for a response, I turned on my heel and stomped into the theatre.

I missed the part where my dad gave Adrien a comforting pat on the back before he hopped in his vehicle and went back to my house.

* * *

"Tonight's show is going to be insane." Nova said as we explored the venue and worked out entrances and exits.

"Yes...*everyone* is coming tonight." I grabbed a wide, flat dry mop and ran it over the floor to clear off some debris. I felt off in so many ways and I knew Nova could sense it. My mind was on the last few days with Adrien, Tabitha, my dad's odd behavior...I had an intense dislike for not being completely in the loop.

"Stel!" Nova cuffed my arm.

"Hmmm?" I glanced over at her.

"Where's your head? I've been talking to you for the last five minutes."

"Sorry, I'm all tangled up. I am excited about the show, but I have this sinking feeling something bad is going to happen." I ceased cleaning the stage and returned the mop to its corner.

"That's what I just said!" She laughed.

"Oh...see? Even when I'm not listening, we're still on the same page!" We tried to high-five and missed.

"Come on, Stel...we're good to go." She put her fingers to her mouth and let out an ear-piercing whistle, "Family! Your turn up here!"

As we made our way down into the main house, I caught sight of Adrien whispering in a corner with the rest of the *Loft* boys. When I cleared my throat, they all jumped like they'd been caught doing something bad.

"Darling...what's going on?" I slid my arms around his waist and bit his scruffy chin.

He laughed, but it sounded wrong and forced, "Don't be silly, little songbird. We were just strategizing for the show tonight." In an attempt to redirect my suspicions, he pulled me close and kissed me. Damn him if it didn't work like a charm.

Caught up in his heady scent and the silky feel of his lips sliding enticingly against mine, all negative thoughts disappeared from my mind as I reached my hands up to run my fingers through his hair, which had gotten longer over the course of our tour.

Sighing, I tilted my head back to study his face. His lush, green eyes were hazy with desire and his square jaw was dusted with stubble that matched his thick, dark mane. I grinned at him.

"What?" His straight brows arched in question.

"You are one sexy, gorgeous man, Adrien Daniel O'Rourke." I kissed him noisily on the cheek.

He chuckled and took my hand as we strolled outside to find Nova and the guys, but paused just inside the door.

I glanced inquiringly over my shoulder.

"You, my lovely Luce, are the most breathtaking creature I have ever beheld." His voice was raspy with emotion.

I caressed his cheek and rose on my toes to brush my lips over his eyes, nose and lips, "Thank you." I whispered.

He tucked my arm through his and tipped an imaginary hat to me, "Shall we make our way through the food pilgrimage that is Portland, milady?"

"I think we can make a dent in it, good sir!" I curtsied.

Snickering, we gathered the troops and began a walking tour of my home.

18

Adrien was still being cagey, but I opted to table the interrogation until after the show.

In his defense, I reasoned, it *had* been a very odd few days and I couldn't blame him for still being shaken. I just hoped he wasn't feeling emasculated by my heroic rescue.

"Do you want to rest up at my house for a bit before we have to start getting ready for tonight?" I ran my fingers through Adrien's hair, massaging his scalp.

He leaned into my touch, closing his eyes in bliss as we rode the transit bus.

"That sounds like a great idea." He murmured.

Our stop was next, so we disembarked and made our way down my street and skipped up the steps, unsurprised as we were lovingly assaulted by Edgar the moment we crossed the threshold.

I was happy to see the mutual affection that had immediately sprung up between my furry child and the love of my life.

Edgar pressed his burly body into Adrien's legs, begging for scratches, which were provided without hesitation.

"Who's a hamsum boy? Who's a hamsum boy? You are, Edgar!"

My eyes widened as I witnessed the heart-melting display of baby-talk that was happening right in front of me. Adrien's ear-caressing baritone was nowhere to be found.

I hadn't seen my father's car outside and, other than the huffing and happy growls emitting from my pit bull, the house was silent.

"Aydo."

He looked up at me from he crouched position in front of Edgar.

"We've got the house to ourselves." I raised a mischievous brow.

His answering eyebrow waggles made me laugh, "I'll meet you upstairs after I let this guy out real quick."

Adrien stood, cupping the back of my neck for a lingering kiss, "Don't be long."

I stared after him as he strolled up the stairs, stripping off his t-shirt to give me a tantalizing view of his broad shoulders and naturally-tanned, muscular back. I bit my lower lip and groaned.

I literally shook myself free of my lusty brain and walked through to the kitchen to let Edgar out back for a few minutes.

My dog understood my urgency, so didn't dilly-dally he was usually wont to do. He did his business and wiggled back inside to plop down contentedly on his bed in front of the window.

I winked at Edgar and he rewarded me with a wide, doggy grin as I scratched his ears and hurried up to my bedroom to see what Adrien had in store for me.

My breath caught in my chest as I took in his nude form standing in the sunlight streaming in through my sheer curtains. I drank in every line and curve of his chiseled body and smirked as I walked quietly up to him and cupped the firmness of his ass.

He laughed quietly and turned to face me, presenting me with the surprise pleasure of his erection pressing into my abdomen.

"For me?" I asked brightly.

"Only you," he replied in a low tone thickened with arousal.

I grew feverish as he claimed my lips, plunging his tongue into my mouth as his hands roamed freely, stripping me from my clothes. Tipping my head back, he grazed his teeth over my pulse, cupping my breasts and tugging my nipples into aching points.

We maneuvered back onto my bed, our limbs tangled and rubbing against each other. I luxuriated in the feel of his warm skin against mine, heightening the sensations of electricity dancing across my nerves.

Adrien slid a finger past my folds and bit back a moan, "You're ready, Luce."

I gripped his shaft and he gasped, "I need you inside me, Adrien. Now."

He settled between my spread thighs, bracing his forearms on either side of my head and searched my face with a tender expression.

Smoothing his hair away from his face, I put all of my feelings into my answering look.

Sucking my bottom lip gently, Adrien pulled away from me for just a moment.

He moved back to rest against my headboard and held his arms out for me.

I crawled towards him, letting my long hair trail up his legs and over his rigid shaft and grinned saucily as he cursed under his breath.

Taking him in my hand, I straddled his hips and guided him into my dripping heat.

"Fuck, Luce!" He squeezed my hips as my inner muscles gripped him tightly and I began to move in a circular motion.

I arched my back as Adrien's nails made small indentations in my skin and he set his teeth in my shoulder causing me to move more insistently against him. We fit together tightly and perfectly, each small thrust he made sent delicious spasms throughout my system.

His stubble scraped against my chest as he suckled my breasts and slipped a hand between us to flick his thumb over my clit.

I gasped as I rocked back and forth, lifting myself up and dropping down onto his shaft, making him throw his head back so hard he banged his head into the headboard.

We both laughed and I tugged on his hair, bringing his mouth to mine once more, and he held me still.

"Look at me, Luce." His eyes were smoky and I could tell it was taking all of his self-control to try and talk.

I undulated sinuously, feeling the answering jerk of his cock deep inside me and it toyed with the line between pleasure and pain.

He took my face in his hands, his jade gaze searing into mine.

I was captivated, and together we moved unhurriedly but with an intensity I'd never felt before. The ever present burn between us became an inferno as perspiration covered our skin and our loud and unchecked cries echoed through my bedroom as we reached our orgasm together.

We clutched at each other, trembling and panting.

I leaned back in his arms brushing my lips over his eyes and forehead, "You've been holding out on me, Aydo."

The corners of his mouth twitched and he hugged me close, rolling us over so we could snuggle.

"So have you, you minx." He bit my earlobe.

I yawned lustily, "Mmmm...I love you." My eyes were heavier than I realized and I dozed off, not noticing the serious expression on Adrien's face.

* * *

"You're all rosy-cheeked." Nova remarked as I took my spot next to her in front of the makeup mirror.

I slid my eyes over to her reflection, "I'm not the only one, lady."

She dimpled, "Fair enough. I *really* missed my husband."

"He's still acting off." I said, knowing I didn't need to be specific.

"I wouldn't be too worried, Stel. Besides, you need to focus on tonight." She had a head start on me and was already touching up the eyeliner around her false eyelashes.

"Yep, you're right. It's been an amazing time, though, hasn't it?" I looked up at nothing in particular, smiling to myself at the adventure we'd made it through.

"No words to express it. But, I am definitely glad to be home and I'm ready to work on our new ideas." She stood up and began putting on her costume.

"Word. I'm very ready for the next part of our journey. Thank you for dancing with me and, you know, everything else." I looked down as a wash of emotion rolled over me.

Nova tugged on my arm to get me standing, then enveloped me in a tight hug. "No one else I'd rather be here with. I'm proud to dance with you...and everything else. I love you."

"Love you." I sniffed and sat back down, pulling my hair back to begin my stage makeup routine for the last time on this tour.

* * *

Moved beyond speech, I stood next to Nova in line with the rest of our group as the audience cheered and applauded in a standing ovation.

I saw Adrien off to the side with the rest of *Loft* and he was beaming with pride.

Not one mistake had been made that night. As far as shows went, this last one had been damn near flawless.

Loft had been our opener that evening, so it was like a two-for-one concert. I, of course, had joined *Loft* to sing and dance as I had done since that first time in New Orleans.

Grinning, we all took one final bow and exited the stage.

"Party time!" Everyone cheered and we all packed up in record time to head back to our dance studio for a celebratory evening.

* * *

Our festivities continued until the wee hours, but I finally got the last of our friends in cabs and on their way home.

My dad rested his arm around my shoulders, "Kiddo, I am so proud of you."

I smiled up at him sleepily and leaned into his side, "Thanks, Daddy. I'm glad you're here."

He kissed the top of my head, "Me too. We'll head out tomorrow afternoon, though. Get some sleep, baby girl." And with that, he collected Alice and they walked across the yard and into the house.

Nova and Rhys waved over their shoulders at me as they, too, headed off to their own home just across the street.

The boys were in various odd positions, fast asleep in the lounge area of the studio, so Adrien and I silently agreed to let them be.

"I'm not ready to leave yet," he complained as we headed inside to go to bed.

I elbowed him playfully, "You're welcome to stay out here with the guys."

Adrien's answer was a swat to my rump, "You know what I mean, Luce."

We got ready for bed together in my en suite. I liked the normalcy of it as we washed our faces and brushed our teeth. I made sure he moisturized, which translated to him standing and sighing impatiently while I smoothed night cream onto his face.

We tumbled naked into bed and dislodged Mata from her spot on my pillow. She was not easily deterred, however, and simply curled up in the crook behind Adrien's legs as he spooned behind me. Edgar was resting comfortably by the footboard.

"I smell like a blueberry." Adrien grumbled, his hot breath tickling my ear.

"You smell delicious and like someone who takes care of their skin. Good night, love." I turned my head to kiss him.

He kissed me back lazily, nuzzling my neck and squeezing me close.

"Good night, little songbird."

19

We saw my dad and Alice off, and then relaxed over a late brunch in my back yard. Andy had cooked everything. I was starting to think I should keep him around as a personal chef and house-boy.

I said as much, which earned a rare laugh from Andy and a light spanking from Adrien. That gave me ideas for later exploration.

"Are you sure you can't come with us, Luce? It won't be the same without you as part of the band." Kyle pleaded as he stuffed more bacon into his mouth.

Adrien seemed particularly interested in my answer, which was, "Well, I would love to, but I have too many responsibilities here at home. I need to rest, for one. For two, it's only four weeks...and then, if I'm not mistaken, you guys were already discussing making a move up here, right?"

Toko replied for all of them, "Yes. We were hoping you'd be able to help with our housing situation. Not letting us move in here, but helping us find a place."

I smiled mysteriously and each of them exchanged a nervous look.

"I want to show you something." Standing, I gestured for all of them to follow me towards the studio. We made our way around the back to a set of stairs.

I unlocked the door at the top and flipped on the lights, "We finished this off when we converted the garage to a studio. It's yours for as long as you need it."

Four surprised faces looked back at me before they checked out the spacious apartment my dad helped me create above my studio.

I crossed my arms over my chest and looked at it as well, smiling proudly. The garage had already been quite large with extra storage space and the like, so the space above it was very roomy. We left the beams exposed and finished off the slanting ceilings with excellent insulation, skylights and cedar. It was styled like an industrial loft with an open floor-plan, four modest-sized bedrooms, a full bath and a half bath, a kitchen, and a central living room area. As soon as

Adrien had confessed their plans to move to Portland, I had every intention of offering this place to them.

"It's even furnished? Luce, you're awesome!" Kyle grabbed me up in a bear hug.

"There's access to the studio from inside in that corner," I pushed him off with a laugh and pointed to a circular hole in the floor which led to a wrought-iron spiral staircase. "Of course, when I'm working in there, you wouldn't be able to come in that way, but there's plenty of space in the lounge down there where we could set up your instruments if you like. It's more room than Nova and I need so…" I trailed off as I caught Adrien staring at me.

"What?" My question ended in a squeak as he swooped in and twirled me around.

"Why didn't you say anything about this place?"

I shrugged, "I wanted it to be a surprise."

He shook his head in disbelief, "Thank you." He dipped his head, plundering my mouth.

Several breathless moments passed before we were interrupted by whooping and hollering.

"Get a room!"

We broke apart, smiling sheepishly.

Hands joined, we all left the apartment and headed back into the house so the boys could start packing up their belongings to make their way to Seattle.

My dad offered to put them up while they were there, but I wasn't sure what they had decided on that point.

* * *

"It's only four weeks and I'll be there for your big finale show, okay?" I stood outside the van with my arms folded in the open driver's side window.

Adrien nodded, "I know. This time just feels different and I don't know why." He tilted his head and brushed my lips across his, inhaling deeply of his scent to keep me company until we were together again.

"Well, it *is* different, Aydo. This time, when the tour ends, we start our life together." I ran my fingers over his light, dusky beard.

"I like the sound of that. 'Our life'". He tugged on a loose strand of my hair and gave me one last kiss before I stepped away from the van.

"I love you, Aydo." I called.

"I love you most, little songbird."

He pulled away from the curb and the boys hung out the windows waving at me until they disappeared around a corner.

My heart was heavy, because I already missed all of them, but hopeful.

With a deep breath, I headed back in the house to grab Edgar and go for a run.

* * *

Thankfully, time flew by. Nova and I had spent it working on new choreography concepts and costume designs while getting back to our normal teaching routines.

I had also enlisted some help from her and Rhys to rearrange some things in the studio so the guys could bring in their instruments when they made the move to Portland.

Adrien and I talked every day, just as we had on the tour when we were apart. His spirits seemed improved from the strange mood he'd been in before he left.

"You don't have to come with me, Vava." I repeated as we loaded up my turquoise Mini Cooper so Rhys could drive us to the airport.

"Of course I do!" She swatted at me from the passenger seat but I dodged her in the back.

We only had carry-on luggage, so Rhys dropped us at the terminal and I thanked him again for watching Mata and Edgar for the few days we would be gone.

"No problem; be safe."

I turned away so Nova could give her husband a proper goodbye, only looking when I felt her arm link through mine.

"Ready, bebe?" She batted her lashes.

"First class tickets—thanks, Daddy—here we come!"

* * *

-Don't freak out; Kyle is picking you up.

This was the first thing I saw after we landed in San Diego and I turn on my phone. I typed out a reply.

-I'm not going to freak out. Are you okay?

My phone vibrated and Adrien's face came on the screen.

"Hey—" but he cut me off.

"I'm sorry, Luce! My car died and I'm at the garage waiting for it to be fixed."

I laughed, "That sounds familiar. It's fine, love. I think I see Kyle. Will you be at the house when we get there?" Nova had my elbow and steered me through to the exit where Kyle waited for us.

"Yes, I think they just finished up. I'll see you soon! I love you," I heard the smile in his voice.

"I love you...see you." I disconnected the call as Kyle jogged up to grab our rolling suitcases.

"Hey, bud!" I gave him a quick hug and he fist-bumped Nova in greeting.

It was a little warmer and brighter in San Diego and the energy was definitely different from my claimed home of Portland.

We piled into Kyle's Toyota and headed off to more unfamiliar territory.

"You ladies hungry or anything? We don't have much at the house, but I think there was talk of going out later." Kyle drummed his fingers on the steering wheel as he expertly navigated through traffic.

I glanced at Nova in the back and she shrugged and shook her head.

"I think we're okay. Thanks, man." I patted him on the shoulder.

"I apologize in advance for the state the house is in, but we've been busy packing. It's not messy, just cluttered with boxes." He looked at me with a guilty smile.

I waved him off, "Don't even worry about it. I'm sure I've seen worse."

The three of us chatted idly for about thirty more minutes before we pulled up in front of a simple, small, white house on a quiet neighborhood street.

"It's cute!" I proclaimed as we exited the car and Kyle retrieved our bags and carried them into the house.

"Thanks, we've had a great time living here." Toko spoke from the doorway, surprising both Nova and me.

I grinned and gave him a hug, "Hey, T! Missed you, kid!" He gave me a friendly squeeze and high-fived Nova before giving her a sideways hug as well.

The house was stuffed with packing boxes, which gave me a secret thrill because it meant that their coming to Portland was really happening.

Nova and I shared a loaded glance and an excited grin as we set our purses down, kicked off our shoes, and made ourselves at home.

The sound of a car pulling up outside just behind Kyle's had me running to the window, "Oh. My. God."

Adrien swept into the house, searching all over the room until he spied me by the window. I was in his arms in less than a heartbeat and kissing him faster than that.

My soul began to settle and purr once more as his scent and the warmth of his body soothed me.

"I—" he silenced me with his tongue in my mouth and my skin hummed.

Pulling away, I put my finger on his lips, "I cannot believe you still have the Bronco! I should have known when you said it was broken down."

He smiled wickedly and nipped my fingertip.

I rested my head on his chest and he swayed with me, "I didn't think I could miss you more than I did when you moved away, but these last weeks have been a torment."

"I know what you mean, Aydo." I gave him a final embrace before letting go.

He didn't let me get far, weaving his fingers with mine and keeping me close the rest of the evening.

We all went out for dinner that night and turned in relatively early.

Adrien made hard and hot love to me, leaving us both panting and spent, before we fell asleep wrapped up together.

* * *

The show was on Shelter Island and *Loft* was a featured artist at the three-day music festival happening there.

The weather was perfect and Nova and I had special passes to hang out behind the scenes with *Loft* and all of the other musical acts we would see.

The tour had only been a small taste of what life with a musician would be like, but this place? *Holy shit* was all I could come up with.

Loft really had a large fan base in San Diego, so we were constantly being stopped by overly made-up girls and hipster boys that wanted photos or autographs.

I stared wide-eyed at everything, turning to Nova often to mouth "Oh, my gods" every time some squealing human came running up to Adrien or the other guys.

I got bumped and shoved a little. A few girls actually sized me up when they realized I was with Adrien. Now, *that* I found exceptionally hilarious.

We got settled in a private tented area and Nova and I amused ourselves while the boys tested their instruments and did vocal warm-ups.

I was in such a haze of wonderment, that I was completely oblivious to the covert looks the guys were exchanging with each other and Nova.

One of the stage managers popped his head through the opening in the tent, "*Loft*, you're up. Let's get moving."

Crew members came to retrieve the instruments and we formed a line as we left through the backside of the tent and approached the stage.

"This is *huge*," I whispered to Nova.

"That's what she said," She shot back, poking me in the ribs. "Damn, Stel, eat a sandwich!"

I batted her hands away as we climbed the stairs up to the left side of the stage.

Adrien came back to me and gave me a hug, "Stay where I can see you."

"Break a leg, Aydo." I gave him a peck on the forehead.

He winked and gave me a panty-melting smile—if I were wearing panties, that is—and I squeezed my thighs together. He was certainly a force to be reckoned with when he was in rock star-mode.

I smirked as I noted my *Candéo* shirt he wore with his scuffed up Chucks and fitted jeans. I'd helped him with his hair so it fell in smooth waves around his shoulders rather than standing up all over the place.

Nova wrapped her arm around my waist as we watched the magic happen.

"So glad to be back in you, San Diego!" Adrien shouted in the microphone.

Cheers and whistled erupted from the packed grassy area designated for concert attendees.

"We have just spent the last four months on a cross-country tour and this is our last stop!"

More cheers.

"I have a few special people I would like to thank," He held his hand up, shielding his eyes as he appeared to search the crowd.

I frowned in confusion as I followed his gaze out into the crowd.

"That's...that's my dad and Alice." I muttered as I started to walk out onto the stage.

Nova pulled me back, "don't go out there!"

I narrowed my eyes at her, "Did you know they would be here?"

She shrugged, trying to look innocent.

I shook my head at her, looking back towards Adrien who had noticed my little freak out.

He held up a finger, signaling me to wait, so I took a deep breath and sought my patience.

"Mr. and Mrs. MacLean, thank you for coming! Nova, thank you!" He smiled in our direction.

"Last but not least, some of you out there might have been following our online activity whilst we were on our tour. You might also know that I found someone very special. A long, lost love, if you will. Miss Luce MacLean." The crowd roared in excitement as he held his hand out to me.

Glaring in wariness, I went to him, my palms sweating.

"Isn't she beautiful, ladies and gentlemen?" He asked as he took my wrist and kissed my gardenia tattoo.

"What are you up to, Aydo?" I whispered out of the corner of my mouth even as I waved to everyone. I gave a pointed look towards my parents and they blew me kisses.

He nuzzled his lips against my ear, "You'll see. Have a seat." He pulled away and gestured to a stool just to the right of the center microphone.

"If you would indulge me, my friends, I would like to open tonight's performance with a brand new, never-before-heard song I've been working on. How does that sound?" he put his hand up by his ear, pretending to listen for their response.

Of course, they clapped and whistled.

Adrien adjusted his guitar and made eye contact with Kyle, Toko, and Andy. Toko gave the requisite four counts with his drumsticks and the opening strains of their new song filled the air.

It was a ballad, that much I could tell. The melody seemed a little familiar, but I couldn't place it right away.

With one last glance my way, Adrien stepped back to the microphone and began,

You loved me before I deserved it
But hid it so far from me
I broke you to save your life
But breaking you set our love free

Songbird flew far from my arms...
Taking...my heart and soul along
I will never know love like yours again
I will wish eternal for your return...
Songbird flew far from me...

*So much time went by and I thought you were
lost
Disappeared from my sight
I couldn't believe you were standing right
there
I knew then for you I would fight*

*Songbird flew back to my arms
Restoring my heart and soul
I will never know love like yours again
I will cherish your return eternal
Songbird flew back here to me...*

Songbird...please marry me?

I covered my mouth with my hands as Adrien made a smooth turn into a kneeling position in front of me, right hand extended.

I looked down to see a beautiful 1920s style diamond ring twinkling in his open palm.

"Luce." Adrien's voice trembled.

I stared into his earnest, green eyes.

"Will you marry me?" He bit his lip in apprehension.

I was nodding emphatically before I was able to speak, falling off of my stool and into his arms on the floor of the stage.

"Yes!" I whispered fiercely into his hair.

He stood, clutching me in his arms and dangling my feet above the ground.

His kiss was abrupt and loud as his excitement got the better of him and he shouted into the microphone, "She said yes!"

He turned to me once more and grabbed my left hand, sliding the ring home. It fit perfectly.

Just like Adrien and I always fit perfectly.

20

I was floating as I returned to the side of the stage where Nova, and now my parents, waited for me.

Their glee was infectious and I found myself surrounded in a group hug as we all bounced together. Even my big, scary daddy bounced right along with us.

"I have to pee!" I yelled as I worked myself out of our tangle.

"I'll go with you," Nova offered.

I waved her off, "It's right over there; I'll be okay."

I skipped down the steps, humming and smiling as I looked at my ring again, so I didn't notice what was heading my direction at an alarming speed.

I hit the ground hard, but my instincts kicked in and I quickly rolled to my back and brought my arms up in front of my face in time to block the blows from bony fists.

"You bitch!" my attacker—Tabitha—shouted as she tried to pummel me.

I think the skank cracked one of my ribs, I thought angrily as I wondered where the bloody security guards were when I actually needed them.

I relaxed my muscles just enough to let Tabitha think she was winning and it worked like a charm. I almost laughed, but didn't want to give any of my plans away as I waited for just a few more breaths before I sprang into action, hooking my right arm around both of hers, trapping her left foot with my right, thrusting upwards with my hips and flipping her onto her back so I was now in the dominant position. She was caught so off guard, she barely fought back as I rolled her onto her stomach and pinned both of her arms behind her, resting all of my weight on her lower back.

"Tabitha," I spoke through gritted teeth, "We have to stop meeting like this."

"Stel! Hey, we need security over here!" Nova appeared next to us, having decided to accompany me anyway. I was awash in gratitude for her intuition at that very moment.

My dad and Alice came running with two guards in tow. They promptly relieved me of my burden and zip-tied Tabitha's wrists together. She was shouting and crying, but her words were completely unintelligible.

"I am most definitely pressing charges." I said darkly as I stood and dusted myself off.

Adrien jogged up to us, "What's going on? Everyone disappeared...what the fuck, Tabitha?! Luce, baby, are you okay?" He brushed grass and dirt off of me, inspecting me all over.

"I'm okay; she just caught me off guard for a moment. I think my ribs might be cracked." I winced as Adrien's fingers gently probed my side.

I looked over at my father who was speaking quietly with the security guards. They looked completely cowed by him and nodded as they escorted Tabitha away to be handed over to the local authorities.

"Come on, Luce. Let's get out of here." Adrien started to lead me away.

"No way! You have a concert to finish! I'll go over to the First Aid tent." I crossed my arms over my chest and glowered at him.

He tried to win the stare down, but I was too determined and keyed up from my fight; a fight which had ended far too quickly, in my opinion.

Slumping in defeat, he nodded and kissed me tenderly, "We're leaving as soon as we're done, got it?"

I quirked one side of my mouth in a wry grin, "Okay, *Boss*. Go kill it."

* * *

Ribs wrapped, ibuprofen swallowed, and my dignity restored, my parents and Nova brought me back to the stage. I finally got to pee, also.

My dad kept a watchful eye on me, even as he tucked me against his chest, "You handled yourself well, kid."

I sighed, almost tearing up, "Thanks, Daddy."

Loft finished their last song of the evening to raucous cheers and applause and hurried off of the stage where I was handed off from my dad to Adrien's protective embrace.

He hadn't been messing around when he said we would leave immediately as he scooped me up and carried me the rest of the way—I thought about protesting, but it was just too sexy—to the band's old-school Dodge van. They hadn't appreciated my rape-van comments earlier in the day.

"We'll meet you at your house," were my dad's parting words as he led Alice away to find their vehicle.

I was tucked in the back with Adrien, who insisted on holding me in his lap, as we left the festival and made our way back.

* * *

Adrien didn't argue with my decision to file charges against Tabitha. In fact, he kept apologizing for not having done so when she had attacked him in Portland.

"Hey, would you stop?" I stopped him with my hand on his cheek.

"I'm sorry. I just feel responsible." He leaned his forehead against mine.

"Well, you're not. Tabitha is the only responsible party here, okay?" I smoothed my lips over his tense brow.

In the end, we handed over all of the internet evidence of her interactions, including several things that Adrien had concealed from me—like the creepy voicemails we'd be talking about later—as well as informing them of what had happened in Portland.

She would be evaluated and possibly institutionalized, because it was clear that Tabitha was not functioning like a rational human being.

As we watched the police officers drive away, I looked up at my—squee!—fiancé, "So, what do you say we get you ready to move?"

"That's the best idea I've heard since you said you'd marry me." He grinned before taking my lips in a gentle claiming.

"Do you think the doctor was serious when he said I shouldn't have sex for a week?" I asked in a serious tone.

Adrien laughed and dragged me back into the house, firmly turning our back on the past and sprinting towards our future.

Epilogue

Tulsa, Oklahoma – in the not too distant future

Adrien

It's a full moon tonight and our favorite playground is alight with strings of white "fairy lights", as Luce calls them.

Only our close friends and family are assembled here. My parents couldn't make it, but the old bitterness has long since faded once I realized I already had the love and approval of the only person that's ever really mattered to me. And she's going to become my wife tonight.

I can't breathe. Not because I'm nervous—although I feel that—but mostly because I hate wearing ties. I dressed in a three-piece, tailored suit Luce chose for me. I'd wear anything she asked, so long as it meant she would be mine forever.

The air around us crackles and shifts and I feel a tingling sensation down my spine. *She's here.*

Like a goddess in antique lace and shimmering crystals, she appears. Securely escorted on the arm of her father, she comes towards me as the opening strains of our song begin.

I had thought we would write something together for her walk down the aisle, but then we realized the perfect song already existed in the form of John Legend's "All of Me". When we listened to it for the first time, we looked at each other and knew without words that there was no other song in existence better made for our wedding.

What Luce *didn't* know was I had a very special surprise that would start any moment.

She looked nowhere else but my face, so I knew the moment she realized what I had done.

Lisette's smooth, silky soprano joined the piano, *"What would I do without your smart mouth..."*

Lisette. Our teacher. The reason for our first meeting.

Luce's smile widened and she brushed away joyful tears as she laughed and shook her head.

At last, she stood next to me. Her father, who insisted I call him Malcolm now, hugged her gently and placed her hand in mine.

Lisette finished our song and came to stand before us, wearing a purple, hooded robe. I grinned at Luce's expression when she realized Lisette was also our priestess for the hand fasting we were having in place of a traditional wedding ceremony.

I had successfully managed to pull two surprises on her, which was next to impossible.

Lisette beamed up at us and Luce wrapped her in a tight embrace. They whispered things to each other and chuckled, keeping their secrets.

As she took her place next to me once more, she spoke, "Well done, Aydo. Thank you."

Knowing it was too soon—not giving a damn—I kissed her, "You're welcome, little songbird."

We looked at Lisette, who nodded and projected her voice, "Let us begin. Welcome friends and family, to the joining of these two souls, Luce and Adrien."

Nova stepped forward with the binding for our hands, and Luce's eyes filled again.

"Vava, it's *beautiful*, thank you!" She caught her in a one-armed hug.

I looked at the long, strip of fabric and gasped in surprise. It *was* beautiful.

Nova had Swedish roots and had spent time studying some of the old Viking practices when she and Luce went through their medieval reenactment phase. She had card-woven pieces from our logo t-shirts, strands of our hair, and varying shades of greens, blues, purples at our request into a vibrant and symbolic blend that would tether us to one another for eternity.

"Present your hands, Luce's on top of Adrien's." We did so and Lisette began to wrap them.

"Under the loving guidance of the Mother, these two souls are hereby bound. Repeat after me, 'So mote it be'!"

Our small gathering joined us, "So mote it be!"

"Luce and Adrien have written their own vows, which they will now say before all of you."

I smiled down at my almost-wife, "Luce, my little songbird. You believed in me before I even knew who that was. You forgave me for the unforgivable. Here and now, I give myself—mind, heart, body, and soul—entirely to you. I am yours. I will love you, care for you, and protect you until we return to dust. And even beyond. I love you."

Tears glistened on her cheeks and I wiped them away with my unbound hand.

She took a deep breath, "Adrien. You're more courageous than I ever realized. Although sometimes misguided," she winked, "you have always put my wellbeing first. I shall endeavor to do the same for you. From this moment and well past the boundaries of eternity, I am yours. I will love you, care for you, and protect you until we return to dust."

"By the blessings of the Goddess, and the State of Oklahoma," Lisette smirked at the second part, "I pronounce you husband and wife." She removed the wrapping from our hands, folded the binding, and handed us a pewter goblet of blessed wine, from which we each took a drink.

I turned to my wife—*my wife*—and pulled her into my arms, dipping her low as I kissed her, delighting our audience, eliciting cheers and applause.

We stood, holding hands, facing our family and friends.

I felt Luce's eyes on me and I gazed down at her.

"Are you ready for this?" She asked with an impish grin.

I leaned down, resting my forehead against hers, "Ready for anything with you by my side, little songbird."

The End

Songbird Playlist

Don't be a pirate...buy your music!

Music is a huge part of my life and the following list is just a small sample of what I was listening to while I wrote *Songbird*.

"All of Me" – John Legend
"Echo" – Incubus
"Beautiful with You" – Halestorm
"Sex Therapy" – Robin Thicke
"Have a Little Faith in Me" – John Hiatt
"Kiss Me" – Ed Sheeran
"Disappear" – Cary Brothers & Garrison Starr
"Outta My Head" – Adam Oliver
"How Long Will I Love You?" – Ellie Goulding
"Whatever It Takes" – Lifehouse

Note from the author

Dear Reader,

Thank you for reading *Songbird*! This story was a real labor of love and I hope you enjoyed reading about Aydo and Luce.

If you have comments, please don't hesitate to let me know! If you liked what you read, please leave a positive review.

I'm still new at this publishing thing, so be constructive with your critiques.

-*Angeleen*

E-mail: angeleenfraser@gmail.com

Facebook: www.facebook.com/angeleenfraser

Twitter: @angeleenfraser

Website: www.angeleenfraser.com

About the Author

Self-portrait by A. Fraser

A lifelong storyteller, Angeleen filled countless notebooks with short tales ever since she learned how to write. *Songbird* is her second foray into self-publishing in the Indie New Adult genre.

Being a belly dancer, singer, and martial artist keeps her very busy, but during those free moments in between she likes to sit on her grey chaise and cook up new, sexy, romantic stories on her laptop while her two cats lay curled by her feet.

She loves unicorns, puppies, kittens, and long-haired men with scruffy faces who eschew wearing shirts...or pants, really. Rainbows always make her squee with delight and she's not even close to resembling a human being until she's had at least two cups of coffee every morning.

Angeleen shares her life with a tall, dark, and handsome South African winemaker with tattoos and a great butt.

Made in the USA
Lexington, KY
11 June 2014